Mary Hallock Foote

The Cup of Trembling

And other stories

Mary Hallock Foote

The Cup of Trembling
And other stories

ISBN/EAN: 9783337424817

Printed in Europe, USA, Canada, Australia, Japan

Cover: Foto ©Andreas Hilbeck / pixelio.de

More available books at **www.hansebooks.com**

THE CUP OF TREMBLING

AND OTHER STORIES

BY

MARY HAL

BOSTON AND NEW YORK

HOUGHTON, MIFFLIN AND COMPANY

The Riverside Press, Cambridge

1895

CONTENTS

THE CUP OF TREMBLING

I

A MINER of the Cœur d'Alêne was returning alone on foot, one winter evening, from
the town in the gulch to his solitary claim
far up on the timbered mountain-side.

His nearest way was by an unfrequented
road that led to the Dreadnaught, a lofty
and now abandoned mine that had struck
the vein three thousand feet above the
valley, but the ore, being low-grade, could
never be made to pay the cost of transportation.

He had cached his snow-shoes, going
down, at the Bruce boys' cabin, the only
habitation on the Dreadnaught road, which
from there was still open to town.

The snows that camp all summer on the
highest peaks of the Cœur d'Alêne were
steadily working downward, driving the
game before them; but traffic had not

ceased in the mountains. Supplies were
still delivered by pack-train at outlying
claims and distant cabins in the standing
timber. The miner was therefore traveling
light, encumbered with no heavier load than
his personal requisition of tobacco and
whisky and the latest newspapers, which he
circulated in exchange for the wayside
hospitalities of that thinly peopled but
neighborly region.

His homeward halt at the cabin was
well timed. The Bruce boys were just sitting down to supper; and the moon, that
would light his lonelier way across the white
slopes of the forest, would not be visible for
an hour or more. The boys threw wood
upon their low cooking-fire of coals, which
flamed up gloriously, spreading its imme-
morial welcome over that poor, chance suggestion of a home. The supper was served
upon a board, or literally two boards, nailed
shelf-wise across the lighted end of the
cabin, beneath a small window where,
crossed by the squares of a dusty sash, the
austere winter twilight looked in: a sky of
stained-glass colors above the clear heights
of snow; an atmosphere as cold and pure as

the air of a fireless church; a hushed multi-
tude of trees disguised in vestments of snow,
a mute recessional after the benediction has
been said.

Each man dragged his seat to the table,
and placed himself sidewise, that his legs
might find room beneath the narrow board.
Each dark face was illumined on one side
by the fitful fire-glow, on the other by the
constant though fading ray from the window; and, as they talked, the boisterous fire
applauded, and the twilight, like a pale
listener, laid its cold finger on the pane.

They talked of the price of silver, of the
mines shutting down, of the bad times East
and West, and the signs of a corrupt generation; and this brought them to the latest
ill rumor from town — a sensation that had
transpired only a few hours before the
miner's departure, and which friends of the
persons discussed were trying to keep as
quiet as possible.

The name of a young woman was mentioned, hitherto a rather disdainful favorite
with society in the Cœur d'Alène — the
wife of one of the richest mine-owners in the
State.

The " Old Man," as the miners called him, had been absent for three months in London, detained from week to week on the tedious but paramount business of selling his mine. The mine, with its fatalistic millions (which, it was surmised, had spoken for their owner in marriage more eloquently than the man could have spoken for himself), had been closed down pending negotiations for its sale, and left in charge of the engineer, who was also the superintendent. This young man, whose personal qualities were in somewhat formidable contrast to those of his employer, nevertheless, in business ways, enjoyed a high measure of his confidence, and had indeed deserved it. The present outlook was somewhat different. Persons who were fond of Waring were saying in town that " Jack must be off his head," as the most charitable way of accounting for his late eccentricity. The husband was reported to be on shipboard, expected in New York in a week or less; but the wife, without explanation, had suddenly left her home. Her disappearance was generally accounted a flight. On the same night of the young woman's evanishment, Superintendent Waring had relieved himself of his duties and responsibilities, and taken himself off, with the same irrevocable frankness, leaving upon his friends the burden of his excuses, his motives, his whereabouts, and his reputation.

Since news of the double desertion had got abroad, tongues had been busy, and a vigorous search was afoot for evidence of the generally assumed fact of an elopement, but with trifling results.

The fugitives, it was easily learned, had not gone out by the railroad; but Clarkson's best team, without bells, and a bobsleigh with two seats in it had been driven into the stable-yard before daylight on the morning of the discovery, the horses rough and jaded, and white with frozen steam; and Clarkson himself had been the driver on this hard night trip. As he was not in the habit of serving his patrons in this capacity, and as he would give none but frivolous, evasive answers to the many questions that were asked him, he was supposed to be accessory to Waring in his crime against the morals of the camp.

While the visitor enlarged upon the evi-

dence furnished by Clarkson's night ride,
the condition of his horses, and his own
frank lying, the Bruce boys glanced at each
other significantly, and each man spat into
the fire in silence.

The traveler's halt was over.   He slipped
his feet into the straps of his snow-shoes,
and took his pole in hand; for now the
moon had risen to light his path; faint
boreal shadows began to appear on the glis-
tening slopes.   He shuffled away, and his
shape was soon lost in the white depths of
the forest.

The brothers sat and smoked by their
sinking fire, before covering its embers for
the night; and again the small window,
whitening in the growing moonlight, was
like the blanched face of a troubled listener.

"That must have been them last night,
you recollect.   I looked out about two
o'clock, and it *was* a bob-sleigh, crawlin' up
the grade, and the horses had n't any bells
on.   The driver was a thick-set man like
Clarkson, in a buffaler coat.   There was two
on the back seat, a man and woman plain
enough, all muffled up, with their heads
down.   It was so still in the woods I could

have heard if they 'd been talkin' no louder than I be now ; but not a word was spoke all the way up the hill. I says to myself, ' Them folks must be pretty well acquainted, 'less they 're all asleep, goin' along through the woods the prettiest kind of a night, walkin' their horses, and not a word in the whole dumb outfit.' "

" I 'm glad you did n't open your head about it," said the elder brother. " We don't know for certain it was them, and it 's none of our funeral, anyhow. Where, think, could they have been going to, supposin' you was right? Would Jack be likely to harbor up there at the mine ? "

" Where else could they get to, with a team, by this road? Where else could they be safer? Jack 's inside of his own lines up there, and come another big snow the road 'll be closed till spring ; and who 'd bother about them, anyway, exceptin' it might be the Old Man ? And a man that leaves his wife around loose the way he done ain't likely to be huntin' her on snow-shoes up to another man's mine."

" I don't believe Jack 's got the coin to be meanderin' very far just about now," said

the practical elder brother. " He 's staked
out with a pretty short rope, unless he 's
realized on some of his claims. I heard he
was tryin' to dig up a trade with a man
who 's got a mine over in the Slocan country. That would be convenient, over the
line among the Kanucks. I would n't wonder if he 's hidin' out for a spell till he
gathers his senses, and gets a little more
room to turn in. He can't fly far with a
woman like her, unless his pockets are
pretty well lined. Them easy-comers easy-
goers ain't the kind that likes to rough it.
I 'll bet she don't bile his shirts or cook his
dinners, not much."

" It 's a wild old nest up there," said the
younger. and more imaginative as well as
more sympathetic of the brothers — " a wild
road to nowhere, only the dropping-off
place."

" What gets me is that talk of Jack's
last fall, when you was in the Kootenai,
about his intentions to bach it up there this
winter, if he could coax his brother out
from Manitoba to bach with him. I
would n't like to think it of Jack, that he 'd
lie that way, just to turn folks off the scent.

But he did, sure, pack a lot of his books and stuff up to the mine ; grub, too, a lot of it ; and done some work on the cabin. Think he was fixin'. up for a hideout, in case he should need one ? Or wa'n't it anything but a bluff ? "

" Naw," the other drawled impatiently. " Jack's no such a deep schemer as all that comes to. More 'n likely he seen he was workin' the wrong lead, and concluded 't was about time for him to be driftin' in another direction. 'T ain't likely he give in to such foolishness without one fight with himself. And about when he had made up his mind to fire himself out, and quit the whole business, the Old Man puts out for London, stuck on sellin' his mine, and can't leave unless Jack stays with it. And Jack says to himself, ' Well, damn it all, I done what I could ! What is to be will be.' That's about the way I put it up."

" I would n't be surprised," the other assented ; " but what 's become of the brother, if there ever was a brother in it at all ? "

" Why, Lord ! a man can change his mind. But I guess he did n't tell his brother about this young madam he was

lookin' after along with the rest of the Old
Man's goods.   I hain't got nothin' against
Jack Waring; he's always been square
with me, and he's an awful good minin'
man.   I'd trust him with my pile, if it was
millions, but I wouldn't trust him, nor any
other man, with my wife."

"Sho! she was poor stuff; she was light,
I tell ye. Think of some of the women
we've known! Did they need watchin'?
No, sir; it ain't the man, it's the woman,
when it's between a young man and a
married woman. It's her foolishness that
gits away with them both. Girls is different. I'd skin a man alive that set the
town talkin' about my sister like *she's* bein'
talked about, now."

The brothers stepped outside and stood
awhile in silence, regarding the night and
breathing the pure, frosty air of the forest.
A commiserating thankfulness swelled in
their breasts with each deep, clean inspiration. They were poor men, but they were
free men — free, compared with Jack.
There was no need to bar their door, or
watch suspiciously, or skulk away and hide
their direction, choosing the defense of win-

ter and the deathlike silence of the snows to
the observation of their kind.

They stared with awe up the white, blank
road that led to the deserted mine, and they
marveled in homely thinking: " Will it
pay ? " It was " the wrong lead this time,
sure."

The brothers watched the road from day
to day, and took note that not a fresh track
had been seen upon it; not a team, or a
traveler on snow-shoes, had gone up or down
since the night when the bob-sleigh with its
silent passengers had creaked up it in the
moonlight. Since that night of the full
moon of January not another footprint had
broken the smoothness of that hidden track.
The snow-tides of midwinter flowed over it.
They filled the gulch and softly mounting,
snow on snow, rose to the eaves of the little
cabin by the buried road. The Bruce boys
dug out their window ; the hooded roof protected their door. They walked about on
top of the frozen tide, and entered their
house, as if it were a cellar, by steps cut in a
seven-foot wall of snow.

One gray day in February a black dog,
with a long nose and bloodshot eyes, leaped

down into the trench and pawed upon the cabin door. Opening to the sound, the Bruce boys gave him a boisterous welcome, calling their visitor by name. The dog was Tip, Jack Waring's clever shepherd spaniel, a character as well known in the mountains as his master. Indeed, he was too well known, and too social in his habits, for a safe member of a household cultivating strict seclusion ; therefore, when Tip's master went away with his neighbor's wife, Tip had been left behind. His reappearance on this road was regarded by the Bruce boys as highly suggestive.

Tip was a dog that never forgave an injury or forgot a kindness. Many a good bone he had set down to the Bruce boys' credit in the days when his master's mine was supposed to be booming, and his own busy feet were better acquainted with the Dreadnaught road. He would not come in, but stood at the door, wagging his tail inquiringly. The boys were about to haul him into the cabin by the hair of his neck, or shut him out in the cold, when a shout was heard from the direction of the road above. Looking out, they saw a strange young man

on snow-shoes, who hailed them a second
time, and stood still, awaiting their response.
Tip appeared to be satisfied now; he briskly
led the way, the boys following, up the frozen
steps cut in their moat-wall of snow, and
stood close by, assisting, with all the eloquence his honest, ugly phiz was capable of,
at the conference that ensued. He showed
himself particularly anxious that his old
friends should take his word for the stranger
whom he had introduced and appeared to
have adopted.

Pointing up the mountain, the young man
asked, " Is that the way to the Dreadnaught
mine ? "

" There ain't anybody workin' up there
now," Jim Bruce replied indirectly, after a
pause in which he had been studying the
stranger's appearance. His countenance
was exceedingly fresh and pleasing, his age
about twenty years. He was buttoned to
the chin in a reefing-jacket of iron-gray Irish
frieze. His smooth, girlish face was all over
one pure, deep blush from exertion in the
cold. He wore Canadian snow-shoes strapped
upon his feet, instead of the long Norwegian
skier on which the men of the Cœur d'Alène

make their winter journeys in the mountains; and this difference alone would have marked him for a stranger from over the line. After he had spoken, he wiped away the icy moisture of his .breath that frosted his upper lip, stuck a short pipe between his teeth, drew off one mitten and fumbled in his clothing for a match. The Bruce boys supplied him with a light, and as the fresh, pungent smoke ascended, he raised his head and smiled his thanks.

"Is this the road to the Waring mine — the Dreadnaught?" he asked again, deliberately, after a pull or two at his pipe.

And again came the evasive answer: "Mine's shut down. Ain't nobody workin' up there now."

The youngster laughed aloud. "Most uncommunicative population I ever struck," he remarked, in a sort of humorous despair. "That's the way they answered me in town. I say, is this a hoodoo? If my brother is n't up there, where in the devil is he? All I ask is a straight answer to a straight question."

The Bruce boys grinned their embarrassment. "You'll have to ask us somethin' easier," they said.

" This is the road to the mine, ain't it ? "

" Oh, that 's the road all right enough," the boys admitted ; " but you can see yourself how much it 's been traveled lately."

The stranger declined to be put off with such casual evidence as this. " The wind would wipe out any snow-shoe track ; and a snow-shoer would as soon take across the woods as keep the road, if he knew the way."

" Wal," said Jim Bruce, conclusively, " most of the boys, when they are humpin' themselves to town, stops in here for a spell to limber up their shins by our fire ; but Jack Waring hain't fetched his bones this way for two months and better. Looks mighty queer that we hain't seen track nor trace of him if he 's been livin' up there since winter set in. Are you the brother he was talkin' of sending for to come out and bach it with him ? "

The boys were conscious of their own uneasy looks as the frank eyes of the stranger met theirs at the question.

" I 'm the only brother he 's got. He wrote me last August that he 'd taken a fit of the sulks, and wanted me to come and

help him work it off up here at his mine. I
was coming, only a good job took me in tow;
and after a month or so the work went back
on me, and I wrote to Jack two weeks ago
to look out for me; and here I am. And
the people in town, where he's been doing
business these six years, act as if they dis-
tantly remembered him. 'Oh, yes,' they say,
'Jack Waring; but he's gone away, don't
you know? Snowed under somewhere;
don't know where.' I asked them if he'd
left no address. Apparently not. Asked
if he'd seemed to be clothed in his proper
senses when last seen. They thought so. I
went to the post-office, expecting to find his
mail piled up there. Every scrap had been
cleaned up since Friday last; but not the
letter I wrote him, so he can't be looking
for me. The P. M. squirmed, like everybody else, when I mentioned my brother;
but he owned that a man's mail can't leave
the box without hands, and that the hands
belonged usually to some of the boys at the
Mule Deer mine. Now, the Mule Deer is
next neighbor to the Dreadnaught, across
the divide. It's a friendly power, I know;
and that confirms me that my brother has

done just what he said he was going to do.
The tone of his letter showed that he was
feeling a bit seedy. He seemed to have
soured on the town for some reason, which
might mean that the town has soured on him.
I don't ask what it is, and I don't care to
know, but something has queered him with
the whole crowd. I asked Clarkson to let
me have a man to show me the way to the
Dreadnaught. He calmly lied to me a blue
streak, and he knew that I knew he was
lying. And then Tip, here, looked me in
the eye, with his head on one side, and I
saw that he was on to the whole business."

"Smartest dog that ever lived!" Jim
Bruce ejaculated. "I would n't wonder if
he knew you was Jack's brother."

"I won't swear that he could name the
connection; but he knows I 'm looking for
his master, and he 's looking for him too;
but he 's afraid to trail after him without
a good excuse. See? I don't know what
Tip 's been up to, that he should be left with
a man like Clarkson; but whatever he 's
done, he 's a good dog now. Ain't you, Tip?"

"*He* done!" Jim Bruce interrupted
sternly. "Tip never done nothing to be

punished for. Got more sense of what's
right than most humans, and lives up to it
straight along. I'd quar'l with any man
that looked cross at that dog. You old
brute, you rascal! What you doin' up
here? Ain't you 'shamed, totin' folks 'way
up here on a wild-goose chase? What you
doin' it fer, eh? Pertendin' you 're so
smart! You know Jack ain't up here;
Jack ain't up here, I say. Go along with
ye, tryin' to fool a stranger!"

Tip was not only unconvinced by these
unblushing assertions on the part of a friend
whose word he had never doubted : he was
terribly abashed and troubled by their mani-
fest disingenuousness. From a dog's point
of view it was a poor thing for the Bruce
boys to do, trying to pass upon him like this.
He blinked apologetically, and licked his
chaps, and wagged the end of his tail, which
had sunk a trifle from distress and embarrassment at his position.

The three men stood and watched the
workings of his mind, expressed in his humble, doggish countenance ; and a final ad-
mission of the truth that he had been trying to conceal escaped Jim Bruce in a burst

of admiration for his favorite's unswerving sagacity.

"Smartest dog that ever lived!" he repeated, triumphant in defeat; and the brothers wasted no more lies upon the stranger.

There was something uncanny, thought the young man, in this mystery about his brother, that grew upon him and waxed formidable, and pursued him even into the depths of the snow-buried wilderness. The breath of gossip should have died on so clean an air, unless there had been more than gossip in it.

The Bruce boys ceased to argue with him on the question of his brother's occupancy of the mine. They urged other considerations by way of delaying him. They spoke of the weather; of the look of snow in the sky, the feeling of snow in the air, the yellow stillness of the forest, the creeping cold. They tried to keep him over night, on the offer of their company up the mountain in the morning, if the weather should prove fit. But he was confident, though graver in manner than at first, that he was going to a supper and a bed at his brother's camp, to say nothing of a brother's welcome.

" I 'm positive he 's up there.   I froze on
to it from the first," he persisted.   " And
why should I sleep at the foot of the hill
when my brother sleeps at the top ? "

The Bruce boys were forced to let him go
on, with the promise, merely allowing for the
chance of disappointment, that if he found
nobody above he would not attempt to return after nightfall by the Dreadnaught
road, which hugs the peak at a height above
the valley where there is always a stiff gale
blowing, and the combing drifts in midwinter are forty feet high.

" Trust Tip," they said ; " he 'll show you
the trail across the mountain to the Mule
Deer " — a longer but far safer way to
shelter for the night.

" Tip is fly ; he 'll see me through," said
Jack's brother.   " I 'd trust him with my
life.   I 'll be back this way possibly in the
morning ; but if you don't see me, come up
and pay us a visit.   We 'll teach the Dreadnaught to be more neighborly.   Here 's
hoping," he cried, and the three drank in
turn out of the young fellow's flask, the
Bruce boys almost solemnly as they thought
of the meeting between the brothers, the

sequel to that innocent hope. Unhappy brother, unhappy Jack!

He turned his face to the snows again, and toiled on up the mountain, with Tip's little figure trotting on ahead.

" Think of Jack's leavin' a dog like that, and takin' up with a woman!" said Jim Bruce, as he squared his shoulders to the fire, yawning and shuddering with the chill he had brought with him from outside. " And such a woman!" he added. " I 'd want the straight thing, or else I 'd manage to git along without. Anything decent would have taken the dog too."

" 'T was mortal cute, though, of the youngster to freeze on to Tip, and pay no attention to the talk. He knows a dog, that 's sure. And Tip knowed him. But I wish we could 'a' blocked that little rascal's game. 'T was too bad to let him go on."

" I never see anybody so stuck on goin' to a place," said the elder Bruce. " We 'll see him back in the morning : but I 'll bet he don't jaw much about brother Jack."

The manager's house at the Dreadnaught had been built in the time of the

mine's supposititious prosperity, and was
the ideal log cabin of the Cœur d'Alêne.
A thick-waisted chimney of country rock
buttressed the long side-wall of peeled logs
chinked with mud. The front room was
twenty feet across, and had a stone hearth
and a floor of dressed pine. Back of it
were a small bedroom and a kitchen into
which water was piped from a spring higher
up on the mountain. The roof of cedar
shakes projected over the gable, shading
the low-browed entrance from the sun in
summer, and protecting it in winter from
the high-piled snows.

Like a swallow's nest it clung in the
hollow of the peak, which slopes in vast,
grand contours to the valley, as if it were
the inside of a bowl, the rim half broken
away. The valley is the bottom of the
bowl, and the broken rim is the lower range
of hills that completes its boundary. Great
trees, growing beside its hidden streams
far below, to the eye of a dweller in the
cabin are dwarfed to the size of junipers,
and the call of those unseen waters comes
dreamily in a distant, inconstant murmur,
except when the wind beats up the peak,

which it seldom does, as may be seen by the warp of the pines and tamaracks, and the drifting of the snows in winter.

To secure level space for the passage of teams in front of the house, an embankment had been thrown up, faced with a heavy retaining-wall of stone. This bench, or terrace, was now all one with the mountain-side, heaped up and smoothed over with snow.

Jack, in his winter nest-building, had cleared a little space for air and light in front of each of the side windows, and with unceasing labor he shoveled out the snow which the wind as constantly sifted into these pits, and into the trench beneath the hooded roof that sheltered the gable entrance.

The snow walls of this sunken gallery rose to the height of the door-frame, cutting out all view from without or within. A perpetual white twilight, warmed by the glow of their hearth-fire, was all that the fugitives ever saw of the day. Sun, or stars were alike to them. One link they had with humanity, however, without which they might have suffered hardship, or even have been forced to succumb to their savage isolation.

The friendly Mule Deer across the mountain was in a state of winter siege, like the Dreadnaught, but had not severed its connections with the world. It was a working mine, with a force of fifty or more men on its pay-roll, and regular communication on snow-shoes was had with the town. The mine was well-stocked as well as garrisoned, and Jack was indebted to the friendship of the manager for many accustomed luxuries which Esmée would have missed in the new life that she had rashly welcomed for his sake. No woman could have been less fitted than she, by previous circumstances and training, to take her share of its hardships, or to contribute to its slender possibilities in the way of comfort. A servant was not to be thought of. No servant but a Chinaman would have been impersonal enough for the situation, and all heathen labor has been ostracized by Christian white labor from the Cœur d'Alène.

So Jack waited upon his love, and was inside man and outside man, and as he expressed it, "general dog around the place." He was a clever cook, which goes without saying in one who has known good living, and has lived eight years a bachelor on the frontier: but he cleaned his own kitchen and washed his own skillets, which does not go without saying, sooner than see Esmée's delicate hands defiled with such grimy tasks. He even swept, as a man sweeps; but what man was ever known to dust? The house, for all his ardent, unremitting toil, did not look particularly tidy.

Its great, dark front room was a man's room, big, undraped and uncurtained, strongly framed, — the framework much exposed in places, — heavy in color, hard in texture, yet a stronghold, and a place of absolute reserve: a very safe place in which to lodge such a secret as Esmée. And there she was, in her exotic beauty, shivering close to a roaring fire, scorching her cheeks that her silk-clad shoulders might be warm. She had never before lived in a house where the fires went out at night, and water froze beside her bed, and the floors were carpetless and cold as the world's indifference to her fate. She was absolutely without clothing suited to such a change, nor would she listen to sensible, if somewhat unattractive, suggestions from Jack. Now, least of all times, could she afford to disguise her picturesque beauty for the sake of mere comfort and common sense, or even to spare Jack his worries about her health.

It was noon, and the breakfast-table still stood in front of the fire. Jack, who since eight o'clock had been chopping wood and "packing" it out of the tunneled snow-drift which was the woodshed into the kitchen, and cooking breakfast, and shoveling snow out of the trenches, sat glowing on his side of the table, farthest from the fire, while Esmée, her chair drawn close to the hearth, was sipping her coffee and holding a fan spread between her face and the flames.

"Jack, I wish you had a fire-screen — one that would stand of itself, and not have to be held."

"Bless you! I'd be your fire-screen, only I think I'm rather hotter than the fire itself. I insist that you take some exercise, Esmée. Come, walk the trench with me ten rounds before I start."

"Why do you start so early?"

" Do you call this early ? Besides, it looks like snow."

" Then, why go at all ? "

" You know why I go, dearest. The boys went to town yesterday. I 've had no mail for a week."

" And can't you exist without your mail ? "

" Existence is just the hitch with us at present. It 's for your sake I cannot afford to be overlooked. If I fall out of step in my work, it may take years to get into line again. I can't say like those ballad fellows :

'Arise! my love, and fearless be,
For o'er the southern moors I have a home for thee.'

" I wish I had. We 'll put some money in our purse, and then we 'll make ourselves a home where we please. Money is the first thing with us now. You must see that yourself."

" I see it, of course ; but it does n't seem the nearest way to a fortune, going twice a week on snow-shoes to play solo at the Mule Deer mine. Confess, Jack dear, you do not come straight away as soon as you get your mail."

"I do not, of course. I must be civil, after a fashion, to Wilfrid Knight, considering all that he is doing for me."

"What is he doing for you?"

"He's working as hard as he can for me in certain directions. It's best not to say too much about these things till they've materialized; but he has as strong a backing as any man in the Cœur d'Alêne. To tell you the truth, I can't afford *not* to be civil to him, if it meant solo every day in the week."

Esmée smiled a little, but remained silent. Jack went around to the chimney-piece and filled his pipe, and began to stalk about the room, talking in brief sentences as he smoked.

"And by the way, dearest, would you mind if he should drop in on us some day?" Jack laughed at his own phrase, so literally close to the only mode of gaining access to their cellarage in the snow.

Esmée looked up quickly. "What in the world does he want to come here for? Does n't he see enough of you as it is?"

"He wants to see something of you; and it's howling lonesome at the Mule Deer. Won't you let him come, Esmée?"

" Why, do you want him, Jack?"

" I want him! What should I want him for? But we have to be decent to a man who's doing everything in the world for us. We couldn't have made it here, at all, without the aid and comfort of the Mule Deer."

" I 'd rather have done without his aid and comfort, if it must be paid for at his own price."

" Everything has got to be paid for. Even that inordinate fire, which you won't be parted from, has to be paid for with a burning cheek."

" Not if you had a fire-screen, Jack," Esmée reminded him sweetly.

" We will have one — an incandescent fire-screen on two legs. Will two be enough? A Mule Deer miner shall pack it in on his back from town. But we shall have to thank Wilfrid Knight for sending him. Well, if you won't have him here, he can't come, of course ; but it 's a mistake, I think. We can't afford, in my opinion, not to see the first hand that is held out to us in a social way — a hand that can help us if it will, but one that is quite as strong to injure us."

" Have him, then, if he's so dangerous. But is he nice, do you think?"

" He's nice enough, as men go. We're not any of us any too nice."

" Some of you are at least considerate, and I think it very inconsiderate of Mr. Wilfrid Knight to wish to intrude himself on me now."

" Dearest, he has been kindness itself, and delicacy, in a way. Twice he has sent a special man to town to hunt up little dainties and comforts for you when my prison fare" —

" Jack, what do you mean? Has Wilfrid Knight been putting his hand in his pocket for things for me to eat and drink?"

" His pocket's not much hurt. Don't let that disturb you; but it is something to send a man fifteen miles down the mountain to pack the stuff. You might very properly recognize that, if you chose."

" I recognize nothing of it. Why did you not tell me how it was? I thought that you were sending for those things."

" How can I send Knight's men on my errands, if you please? I don't show up very largely at the mine in person. You

don't seem to realize the situation. Did
you suppose that the Mule Deer men, when
they fetch these things from town, know
whom they are for? They may, but they
are not supposed to."

"Arrange it as you like, but I will not
take presents from the manager of the Mule
Deer."

"He has dined at your table, Esmée."

"Not at *my* table," said Esmée, haughtily
averting her face.

"But you have been nice to him; he remembers you with distinct pleasure."

"Very likely. It is my rôle to be nice
to people. I should be nice to him if he
came here now; but I should hate him for
coming. If *he* were nice, he would not
dream of your asking him or allowing him
to come."

"Darling, darling, we can't keep it up
like this. We are not lords of fate to that
extent. Fellows will pay you attention;
they always have and they always will: but
you must not, dearest, imply that I am not
sensitive on the point of what you may or
may not receive in that way. I should
make myself a laughing-stock before all men

if I should begin by resenting things. I
could not insult you so. I will resent nothing that a husband does not resent."

"Jack, don't you understand? I could
have taken it lightly once; I always used
to. I can't take it lightly now. I cannot
have him come here — the first to see us in
this *solitude à deux*, the most intimate, the
most awful — "

"Of course, of course," murmured Jack.
"It is awful, I admit it, for you. But it
always will be. Ours is a double solitude
for life, with the world always eying us
askance, scoring us, or secretly envying us,
or merely wondering coarsely about us. It
takes tremendous courage in a woman; but
you will have the courage of your honesty,
your surpassing generosity to me."

"Generosity!" Esmée repeated. "We
shall see. I give myself just five years of
this 'generosity.' After that, the beginning
of the end. I shall have to eliminate myself
from the problem, to be finally generous.
But five years is a good while," she whispered, "to dare to love my love in, if my
love loves me."

There could be no doubt of this as yet.

Esmée could afford to toy sentimentally with the thought of future despair and final self-elimination.

" Come, come," said Waring; " this will never do; we must get some fresh air on this." He knocked the ashes out of his pipe, pocketed it, and marched into an inner room whence he fetched a warm, loose cloak and a pair of carriage boots.

" Fresh air and exercise ! "

Esmée, seeing there was to be no escape from Jack's favorite specific for every earthly ill, put out her foot, in its foolish little slipper, and Jack drew on the fur-lined boots, and laced them around the silken ankles.

He followed her out into the snow-walled fosse, and fell into step beside her.

" May I smoke ? "

" What affectation ! As if you did n't always smoke."

" Well, hardly, when I have a lady with me, in such a public place."

" Oh me, oh me ! " Esmée suddenly broke forth, " why did I not meet you when you were in New York the winter before ! Well,

it would have settled one or two things.
And we might be walking like this now,
before all the world, and every one would
say we were exactly suited to each other.
And so we are — fearfully and wonderfully.
Why did that fact wait to force itself upon
us when to admit it was a crime? And we
were so helpless *not* to admit it. What resources had I against it?"

"God knows. Perhaps I ought to have
made a better fight, for your sake. But the
fight was over for me the moment I saw that
you were unhappy. If you had seemed
reasonably content with your life, or even
resigned, I hope I should have been man
enough to have taken myself off and had it
out alone."

"I had no life that was not all a pretense
and a lie. I began by thinking I could
pretend to you. But you know how all that
broke down. Oh, Jack, *you* know the
man!"

"I would n't go on with that, Esmée."

"But I must. I must explain to you just
once, if I can."

"You need not explain, I should hope, to
me."

" But this is something that rankles fearfully. I must tell you that I never, never would have given in if I had n't thought there was something in him, really. Even his peculiarities at first seemed rather picturesque ; at least they were different from other men's. And we thought him a great original, a force, a man of such power and capacity. His very success was supposed to mean that. It was not his gross money that appealed to me. You could not think that I would have let myself be literally sold. But the money seemed to show what he had done. I thought that at least my husband would be a man among men, and especially in the West. But " —

" Darling, need we go into all this ? Say it to yourself, if it must be said. You need not say it to me."

" *I* am saying it, not you. It is not you who have a monstrous, incredible marriage to explain. I must explain it as far as I can. Do you think I can afford to be without your respect and comprehension simply because you love me ? "

" But love includes the rest."

" Not after a while. Now let me speak.

It was when he brought me out here that I
saw him as he is. I measured him by the
standards of the life that had made him. I
saw that he was just a rough Western man,
like hundreds of others; not half so picturesque as a good many who passed the
window every day. And all his great success, which I had taken as a proof of ability,
meant nothing but a stroke of brutal luck
that might happen to the commonest miner
any day. I saw how you pretended to
respect his judgment while privately you
managed in spite of it. I could not help
seeing that he was laughed at for his preten-
sions in the community that knew him best.
It was tearing away the last rag of self-
respect in which I had been trying to dress
up my shameful bargain. I knew what you
all thought of him, and I knew what you
must think of me. I could not force myself
to act my wretched part before you; it
seemed a deeper degradation when you were
there to see. How could I let you think
that *that* was my idea of happiness! But
from the first I never could be anything
with you but just myself — for better or for
worse. It was such a rest, such a perilous

rest, to be with you, just because I knew it was no use to pretend. You always seemed to understand everything without a word."

" I understood *you* because I gave my whole mind to the business. You were in my thoughts night and day, from the moment I first saw you."

" Yes," said Esmée, passing over this confession as a thing of course in a young man's relations with his employer's wife. " It was as if we had been dear friends once, before memory began, before anything began ; and all the rest came of the miserable accident of our being born — mis-born, since we could not meet until it was too late. Oh, it was cruel ! I can never forgive life, fate, society — whatever it was that played us this trick. I had the strangest forebodings when they talked about you, before I saw you — a premonition of a crisis, a danger ahead. There was a fascination in the commonest reports about you. And then your perfectly reckless naturalness, of a man who has nothing to hide and nothing to fear. Who on earth could resist it ? "

" I was the one who ought to have resisted it, perhaps. I don't deny that I was 'natural.' We're neither of us exactly humbugs — not now. If the law that we've broken is hunting for us, there will be plenty of good people to point us out. All that we shall have to face by and by. I wish I could take your share and mine too; but you will always have it the harder. That, too, is part of the law, I suppose."

"I must not be too proud," said Esmée. "I must remember what I am in the eyes of the world. But, Jack dear, if Wilfrid Knight does come, do not let him come without telling me first. Don't let him 'drop in on us,' as you said."

"He shall not come at all if it bothers you to think of it. I am not such a politic fellow. It's for your sake, dearest one, that I am cringing to luck in this way. I never pestered myself much about making friends and connections; but *I* must not be too proud, either. It's a handicap, there's no doubt about that; it's wiser to accept the fact, and go softly. Great heavens! haven't I got you?"

"I suppose Wilfrid Knight is a man of the world? He'll know how to spare the situation?"

" Quite so," said Jack, with a faint smile.
" You need n't be uneasy about him."
Then, more gravely, he added : —

" He knows this is no light thing with
either of us. He must respect your courage — the courage so rare in a woman —
to face a cruel mistake that all the world
says she must cover up, and right it at any
cost."

" That is nonsense," said Esmée, with the
violence of acute sensitiveness. " You need
not try to doctor up the truth to me. You
know that men do not admire that kind of
courage in women — not in their own women.
Let us be plain with each other. I don't
pretend that I came here with you for the
sake of courage, or even of honesty."

Esmée stopped, and turned herself about,
with her shoulders against the wall of snow,
crushing the back of her head deep into its
soft, cold resistance. In this way she gained
a glimpse of the sky.

" Jack, it does look like a storm. It 's
all over gray, is it not ? and the air is so
raw and chilly. I wish you would not go
to-day."

" I 'll get off at once, and be back before

dark. There shall be no solo this afternoon.
But leave those dishes for me.   I despise to
have you wash dishes."

"I hate it myself.   If I do do it, it will
be to preserve my self-respect, and partly
because you are so slow, Jack dear, and
there's no comfort in life till you get
through. What a ridiculous, blissful, squalid
time it is! Shall we ever do anything
natural and restful again, I wonder?"

"Yes; when we get some money."

"I can't bear to hear you talk so much
about money. Have I not had enough of
money in my life?"

"Life is more of a problem with us than
it is with most people."

"Let us go where nature solves the problem.   There was an old song one of my
nurses used to sing to me —

'Oh, islands there are, in the midst of the deep,
  Where the leaves never fade, and the skies never weep.'

"Can't we go, Jack dear? Let us be
South Sea Islanders. Let's be anything
where there will be no dishes to wash, or
somebody to wash them for us."

"We will go when we get some money,"
Jack persisted hauntingly.

"Oh, hush about the money! It's so un-complimentary of you. I shall begin to think " —

"You must not think. Thinking, after a thing is done, is no use. You must 'sleep, dear, sleep.' I shall be back before dark; but if I am not, don't think it strange. One never knows what may happen."

When he was gone Esmée was seized with a profound fit of dawdling. She sat for an hour in Jack's deep leather chair by the fire, her cloak thrown back, her feet, in the fur boots, extended to the blaze. For the first time that day she felt completely warm. She sat an hour dreaming, in perfect physical content.

Where did those words that Jack had quoted come from, she mused, and repeated them to herself, trying their sound by ear.

"Then sleep, dear, sleep!"

They gathered meaning from some fragmentary connection in her memory.

"If thou wilt ease thine heart
Of love, and all its smart —
Then sleep, dear, sleep!"

"And not a sorrow " —

She could recall no more. The lines had
an echo of Keats. She looked across the
room toward the low shelves where Jack's
books were crammed in dusty banishment.
It was not likely that Keats would be in
that company; yet Jack, by fits and starts,
had been a passionate reader of everybody,
even óf the poets.

She was too utterly comfortable to be
willing to move merely to lay the ghost of
a vanished song. And now another verse
awoke to haunt her : —

> " But wilt thou cure thine heart
> Of love, and all its smart —
> Then die, dear, die ! "

> " 'T is deeper, sweeter " —

Than what ? She could not remember. She
had read the verses long ago, as a girl of
twenty measures time, when the sentiment
had had for her the palest meaning. Now
she thought it not extravagant, but simply
true.

> "Then die, dear, die ! "

She repeated, pillowing her head in the satin
lining of her cloak. A tear of self-forgiving
pity stole down her cheek. Love, — of her

own fair, sensitive self; love of the one who
could best express her to herself, and mag-
nify her day by day, on the highest key of
modern poetic sympathy and primal passion
and mediæval romance, — this was the whole
of life to her. She desired no other revela-
tion concerning the mission of woman. In
no other sense would she have held it worth
while to be a woman. Yet she, of Beauty's
daughters, had been chosen for that stupid-
est of all the dull old world's experiments in
what it calls success — a loveless marriage!

When at length the fire went down, and
the air of the draughty room grew cool, Esmée languidly bestirred herself. The con-
fusion that Jack had left behind him in his
belated departure began to afflict her — the
unwashed dishes on the table, the crumbs on
the floor, the half-emptied pipe and ashes on
the mantel, the dust everywhere. She pitied
herself that she had no one at her command
to set things right. At length she rose,
reluctantly dispensing with her cloak, but
keeping the fur boots on her feet, and began
to pile up the breakfast dishes, and carry
them by separate journeys to the kitchen.

The fire had long been out in the cook-

stove ; the bare little place was distressingly
cold ; neither was it particularly clean, and
the nature of its disorder was even more
objectionable than that of the sitting-room.
Poor Jack! Esmée had profoundly admired
and pitied his struggles with the kitchen.
What man of Jack's type and breeding had
ever stood such a test of devotion? Even
young Sir Gareth, who had done the same
sort of thing, had done it for knighthood's
sake, and had taken pride in the ordeal.
With Jack such service counted for nothing
except as a preposterous proof of his love
for her.

Suppose she should surprise him in house-
wifely fashion, and treat him to a clean
kitchen, a bright fire, and a hot supper on
his return ? The fancy was a pleasing one ;
but when she came to reckon up the un-
avoidable steps to its accomplishment, the
details were too hopelessly repellent. She
did not know, in fact, where or how to begin. She mused forlornly on their present
situation, which, of course, could not last;
but what would come next? Surely, without money, plucked of the world's respect
and charity, they were a helpless pair. Jack

was right; money they must have; and she
must learn to keep her scruples out of his
way; he was sufficiently handicapped already. She hovered about the scene of his
labors for a while, mourning over him, and
over herself for being so helpless to help
him. By this time the sitting-room fire
had gone quite down; she put on a pair of
gloves before raking out the coals and
laying the wood to rebuild it. The room
had still a comfortless air, now that she was
alone to observe it. She could have wept
as she went about, moving chairs, lifting
heavy bearskins, and finding dirt, ever more
dirt, that had accumulated under Jack's
superficial housekeeping.

Her timid attempt at sweeping raised a
hideous dust. When she tried to open the
windows every one was frozen fast, and
when she opened the door the cold air cut
her like a knife.

She gave up trying to overhaul Jack's
back accounts, and contented herself with
smoothing things over on the surface. She
possessed in perfection the decorative touch
that lends an outward grace to the aspect
of a room which may be inwardly unclean,

and therefore unwholesome, for those who live in it.

It had never been required of her that she should be anything but beautiful and amiable, or do anything but contribute her beauty and amiability to the indulgent world around her. The hard work was for those who had nothing else to bestow. She laid Jack's slippers by the fire, and, with fond coquetry, placed a pair of her own little mouse-colored suedes, sparkling with silver embroidery, close beside them. Her velvet wrap with its collar of ostrich plumes she disposed effectively over the back of the hardwood settle, where the shimmering satin lining caught a red gleam from the fire. Then she locked the outer door, and prepared to take Jack's advice, and "sleep, dear, sleep."

At the door of her bedroom she turned for a last survey of the empty room — the room that would live in her memory as the scene of this most fateful chapter of her life. That day, she suddenly remembered, was her younger sister's wedding-day. She would not permit the thoughts to come. All weddings, since her own, were hateful to her. "Hush!" she inwardly breathed, to quell her heart. "The thing was done. All that was left was dishonor, either way. This is my plea, O God! There was no escape from shame! And Jack loved me so!"

About five o'clock of that dark winter day Esmée was awakened from her warm sleep by a loud knocking on the outside door. It could not be Jack, for he had carried with him the key of the kitchen door, by which way he always entered on his return. It was understood between them that in his absences no stranger could be admitted to the house. Guests they did not look for; as to friends, they knew not who their friends were, or if, indeed, they had any friends remaining since their flight.

The knocking continued, with pauses during which Esmée could fancy the knocker outside listening for sounds within the house. Her heart beat hard and fast. She had half risen in her bed; at intervals she drew a deep breath, and shifted her weight on its supporting arm.

Footsteps could be heard passing and re-passing the length of the trench in front of the house. They ceased, and presently a man jumped down into the pit outside her bedroom window; the window was curtained, but she was aware that he was there, trying to look in. He laid his hand on the window-frame. and leaped upon the sill, and shook the sash, endeavoring to raise it; but the blessed frost held it fast. The man had a dog with him, that trotted after him, back and forth, and seconded his efforts to gain entrance by leaping against the door, and whining, and scratching at the lock.

The girl was unspeakably alarmed, there was something so imperative in the stranger's demand. It had for her startled ear an awful assurance, as who should say, " I have a right to enter here." Who was it, what was it, knocking at the door of that guilty house?

It seemed to Esmée that this unappeasable presence had haunted the place for an hour or more, trying windows, and going from door to door. At length came silence so prolonged and complete that she thought herself alone at last.

But Jack's brother had not gone. He was standing close to the window of the outer room, studying its interior in the

strong light and shadow of a pitch-pine fire.
The room was confiding its history to one
who was no stranger to its earlier chapters,
and was keen for knowledge of the rest.

This was Jack's house, beyond a doubt,
and Jack was its tenant at this present time,
its daily intimate inhabitant. In this sense
the man and his house were one.

The Dreadnaught had been Jack's first
important mining venture. In it he had sunk
his share of his father's estate, considerable time and reputation, and the best work
he was capable of ; and he still maintained,
in accordance with his temperament, that
the mine was a good mine, only present conditions would not admit of the fact being
demonstrated. The impregnable nature of
its isolation made it a convenient cache for
personal properties that he had no room for
in his quarters in town, the beloved impedi-
menta that every man of fads and enthu-
siasms accumulates even in a rolling-stone
existence. He was all there: it was Jack
so frankly depicted in his belongings that
his young brother, who adored him, sighed
restlessly, and a blush of mingled emotions
rose in his snow-chilled cheek.

What reminder is so characteristic of a man as the shoes he has lately put off his feet? And, by token, there were Jack's old pumps waiting for him by the fire.

But now suspicion laid its finger on that very unnamed dread which had been lurking in the young man's thoughts. Jack, the silent room confessed, was not living here alone. This could hardly be called " baching it," with a pair of frail little feminine slippers moored close beside his own. Where had Jack's feet been straying lately, — on what forbidden ground, — that his own brother must be kept in ignorance of such a step as this? If he had been mad enough to fetch a bride to such an inhuman solitude as this, — if this were Jack's lawful honeymoon, why should his bliss be hedged about with an awkward conspiracy of silence on the part of all his friends?

The silent room summoned its witnesses; one by one each mute, inanimate object told its story. The firelight questioned them in scornful flashes; the defensive shadows tried to confuse the evidence, and cover it up.

But there were the conscious slippers reddening by the hearth. The costly Paris wrap displayed itself over the back of Jack's honest hardwood settle. On the rough table, covered with a blanket wrought by the hands of an Indian squaw, glimpsed a gilded fan, half-open, showing court ladies, dressed as shepherdesses, blowing kisses to their ephemeral swains. Faded hot-house roses were hanging their heads — shriveled packets of sweetness — against the brown sides of a pot-bellied tobacco-jar, the lid of which, turned upside down, was doing duty as an ash-receiver. A box of rich confectionery imported from the East had been emptied into a Dresden bowl of a delicate, frigid pattern, reminding one of such purebred gentlewomen as Jack's little mother, from whom he had coaxed this bit of the family china on his last home visit.

We do not dress up our brother's obliquity in euphemistic phrases; Jack might call it what he pleased ; but not the commonest man that knew him had been willing to state in plain words the manner of his life at present, snowed in at the top of the Dreadnaught road. Behold how that life spoke for itself: how his books were covered with dust; how the fine, manly rigor of the room had been debased by contact with the habits of a luxurious dependent woman!

Here Jack was wasting life in idleness, in self-banishment, in inordinate affections and deceits of the flesh. The brother who loved him too well to be lenient to his weakness turned away with a groan of such indignant heartbreak as only the young can know. Only the young and the pure in heart can have such faith in anything human as Jack's brother had had in Jack.

Esmée, reassured by the long-continued silence, had ventured out, and now stepped cautiously forward into the broad, low light in the middle of the room. The fireshine touched her upraised chin, her parted lips, and a spark floated in each of her large, dark, startled eyes. Tip had been watching as breathless and as motionless as his companion, but now at sight of Esmée he bounded against the sash, and squealed his impatience to be let in. Esmée shrank back with a cry; her hands went up to her breast and clasped themselves. She had seen the face at the window. Her attitude

was the instinctive expression of her con-
victed presence in that house. And the
excluded pair who watched her were her
natural judges: Fidelity that she had outraged, and Family Affection that she had
wronged.

Tip made further demonstrations at the
window, but Esmée had dragged herself
away out of sight into her own room.

The steps of the knocker were heard, a
few minutes later, wandering irresolutely up
and down the trench. For the last time
they paused at the door.

" Shall we knock once more, Tip? Shall
we give her one more chance ? She has seen
that I am no ruffian; she knows that you
are a friend. Now if she is an honest
woman let her show herself ! For the last
time, then ! "

A terrific peal of knocking shocked the
silence. Esmée could have screamed, there
was an accent so scornfully accusative in
this last ironical summons. No answer was
possible. The footsteps turned away from
the door, and did not come back.

II

The snow that had begun to fall softly and quietly about the middle of the afternoon had steadily increased until now in the thickening dusk it spread a white blindness everywhere. From her bedroom window Esmée looked out, and though she could not see the sky, there were signs enough to tell her what the coming night would be. Fresh snow lay piled in the trench, and snow was whirling in. The blast outside wailed in the chimney, and shook the house, and sifted snow in beneath the outer door.

Esmée was not surprised that Jack, when he came home, should be as dismal and quiet as she was herself; but it did surprise her that he should not at once perceive that something had happened in his absence.

At first there was supper to cook, and she could not talk to him then. Later, when they were seated together at the table, she tried to speak of that ghostly knocking; but Jack seemed preoccupied and not inclined to talk, and she was glad of an excuse to postpone a subject that had for her a peculiar terror in its suggestions.

It was nine o'clock before all the little
house tasks were done, and they drew up
to the fire, seeking in each other's eyes the
assurance that both were in need of, that
nothing of their dear-bought treasure of
companionship had altered since they had
sat that way before. But it was not quite
the same Esmée, nor the same Jack. They
were not thinking exclusively of each other.

" Why don't you read your letters,
dear ? "

" I can't read them," said Esmée.
" They were not written to me — the
woman I am now."

These were the home letters, telling of
her sister's coming wedding festivities, that
Esmée could not read, especially that one
from Lilla — her last letter as a girl to the
sister who had been a bride herself, and
would know what a girl's feelings at such a
time must be.

" I have tried to write to mama," said Esmée ; " but it's impossible. Anything I
could say by way of defense sounds as if I
were trying to lay the blame on some one
else ; and if I say nothing, but just state
the facts, it is harsh, as if I were brazening

it out.   And she has never seen you, Jack. You are my only real defense.   By what you are, by what you will be to me, I am willing to be judged."

"Dearest, you make me ashamed, but I can say the same of you.   Still, to a mother, I'm afraid it will make little difference whether it's 'Launcelot or another.'"

"It certainly made little difference to her when she made her choice of a husband for me," said Esmée, bitterly.   One by one she dropped the sheets of her letters in the fire, and watched them burn to ashes.

"When they know — if they ever write to me after that, I will read those letters. These have no meaning."   They had too much meaning, was what Esmée should have said.

After a silence Jack spoke somewhat hoarsely: "It's a beastly long time since I have written to any of my people.   It's a pity I didn't write and tell them something; it might have saved trouble.   But how can a fellow write?   I got a letter to-day from my brother Sid.   Says he's thinking of coming out here."

"Heaven save us!" cried Esmée.   "Do

write at once — anything — say anything
you like."

Jack smiled drearily. " I 'm afraid it 's
too late. In fact, the letter was written the
day before he was to start, and it 's dated
January 25. There 's a rumor that some
one is in town, now, looking for me. I
should n't be surprised if it were Sid."

" What if it were ? " asked Esmée.
" What could you do ? "

" I don't know, indeed," said Jack.
" I 'm awfully cut up about it. The worst
of it is, I asked him to come."

" You asked him ! "

" Some time ago, dearest, when everything was different. I thought I must
make the fight for both our sakes, and I
sent for Sid, thinking it might help to have
him here with me."

" Did you indeed," said Esmée, coldly.
" What a pity he did not come before it was
too late; he might have saved us both.
How long ago was it, please ? "

" Esmée, don't speak to me like that."

" But do you realize what you are saying ? "

" You should not mind what I say.

Think — what shall we do if it should be Sid? It rests with you, Esmée. Could you bear to meet him?"

"What is he like?" said Esmée, trembling.

"Oh, he's a lovely fellow. There's nobody like Sid."

"What does he look like?"

"He's good-looking, of course, being my brother," said Jack, with a wretched attempt at pleasantry, which met with no response. Esmée was staring at him, a strange terror in her eyes. "But there is more to his looks, somehow, than to most pretty boys. People who are up in such things say he's like the Saint George, or Saint Somebody, by Donatello. He's blond, you know; he's as fresh as a girl, but he has an uncommonly set look at times, when he's serious or a bit disgusted about something. He has a set in his temper, too. I should not care to have Sid hear our story — not till after he had seen you, Esmée. Perhaps even then he could not understand. He has never loved a woman, except his mother. He doesn't know what a man's full-grown passion means. At least, I don't think he knows. He was rather fiercely moral on some points when I talked to him last; a little bit inhuman — what is it, Esmée ? "

" There is that dog again ! "

Jack looked at her in surprise at her shocked expression. Every trace of color had left her face. Her eyes were fixed upon the door.

" What dog ?   Why, it 's Tip."

A creature as white as the storm sprang into the room as he opened the door, threw himself upon Jack, and whimpered and groaned and shivered, and seemed to weep with joy. Jack hugged him, laughing, and then threw him off, and dusted the snow from his clothing.

Tip shook himself, and came back excitedly for more recognition from his master. He took no notice at all of Esmée.

"Speak to him, won't you, dear? It 's only manners, even if you don't care for him," Jack prompted gently. But Tip refused to accept Esmée's sad, perfunctory greeting ; his countenance changed, he held aloof, glancing at her with an unpleasant gleam in his bloodshot eyes.

He had satisfied the cravings of affection,

and now made it plain that his visit was on
business that demanded his master's attention outside of the house. Jack knew the
creature's intelligent ways so well that
speech was hardly needed between them.
" What's the racket, Tip? What's wrong
out there? No, sir; I don't go back to
town with you to-night, sir. Not much.
Lie down! Be quiet, idiot! "

But Tip stood at the door, and began to
whine, fixing his eyes on his master's face.
As nothing came of this, he went back and
stood in front of him, wagging his tail
heavily and slowly; troubled wrinkles stood
out over his beseeching eyes.

" What under heaven's the matter with
you, dog? You're a regular funeral procession." Jack shoved the creature from
him, and again he took up his station at the
door. Jack rose, and opened it, and play-
fully tried to push him out. Tip stood his
ground, always with his eyes on his master's face, and whimpered under his breath
with almost tearful meaning.

" He's on duty to-night," said Jack.
" He's got something on his mind, and
he wants me to help him out with it. I

say, old chap, we don't keep a life-saving station up here. Get out with your nonsense."

"There was some one with him when he was here this afternoon," Esmée forced herself to say.

"Has Tip been here before?"

"Yes, Jack. But a man was with him — a young, strange man. It was about four o'clock, perhaps five; it was getting dusk. I had been asleep, and I was so frightened. He knocked and knocked. I thought he would never stop knocking. He came to my window, and tried to get in, but the sash was frozen fast." Esmée paused, and caught her breath. "And I heard a dog scratching and whining."

"Did you not see the man?"

"I did. I saw him," gasped Esmée. "It was all quiet after a while. I thought he had gone. I came out into the room, and there he stood close by that window, staring in; and the dog was with him. It was Tip."

"And you did not open the door to Tip?"

"Jack dear, have you not told me that I

was never to open the door when you were away?"

"But did n't you speak to the man? Did n't you ask him who he was or what he wanted?"

"How could I? He did not speak to me. He stared at me as if I were a ghost, and then he went away."

"I would have questioned any man that came here with Tip. Tip does n't take up with toughs and hobos. What was he like?"

Esmée had retreated under this cross-questioning, and stood at some distance from Jack, pale, and trembling with an ague of the nerves.

"What was he like?" Jack repeated.

"He was most awfully beautiful. He had a face like — like a death-angel."

Jack rejected this phrase with an impatient gesture. "Was he fair, with blue eyes, and a little blond mustache?"

"I don't know. The light was not good. He stood close to the window, or I could not have seen him. What have I done? Was it wrong not to open the door?"

"Never mind about that, Esmée. I want you to describe the man."

" I can't describe him. I don't need to.
I know — I know it was your brother."

" It must have been ; and we have been
sitting here — how many hours ? "

" I did not know there could be anybody
— who — had a right to come in."

" Such a night as this ? Get away, Tip ! "

Jack had risen, and thrown off his coat.
Esmée saw him get down his snow-shoe rig.
He pulled on a thick woolen jersey, and
buttoned his reefer over that. His foot-
gear was drying by the fire ; he put on a
pair of German stockings, and fastened them
below the knee, and over these the India-
rubber buskins which a snow-shoer wears.

" Tip had better have something to eat
before we start," he suggested. He did
not look at Esmée, but his manner to her
was very gentle and forbearing ; it cut her
more than harsh words and unreasonable
reproaches would have done.

" He seems to think that I have done it,"
she said to herself, with the instinct of self-
defense which will always come first with
timid natures.

Tip would not touch the food she brought
him. She followed him about the room

meekly, with the plate in her hand; but he shrunk away, lifting his lip, and showing the whites of his blood-rimmed eyes.

Except for this defect, the sequel of distemper or some other of the ills of puppyhood, Tip had been a good-looking dog. But this accident of his appearance had prejudiced Esmée against him at the first sight. Later he had made her dislike and fear him by a habit he had of dogging his master to her door, and waiting there, outside, like Jack's discarded conscience. If chidden, or invited to come in, the unaccountable creature would skulk away, only to return and take up his post of dumb witness as before; so that no one who watched the movements of Jack's dog could fail to know how Jack bestowed his time. In this manner Esmée had come almost to hate the dog, and Tip returned her feeling in his heart, though he was restrained from showing it. But to-night there was a new accusation in his gruesome eye.

" He will not eat for me," said Esmée, humbly.

" He must eat," said Jack. " Here, down with it!" The dog clapped his jaws on the meat his master threw to him, and stood ready, without a change of countenance, at the door.

" Can't you say that you forgive me ? " Esmée pleaded.

" Forgive you ? Who am I, to be forgiving people ? " Jack answered hoarsely.

" But say it — say it! It was your brother. If it had been mine, I could forgive you."

" Esmée, you don't see it as it is."

" I do see it ; but, Jack, you said that I was not to open the door."

" Well, you didn't open it, did you ? So it's all right. But there's a man out in the snow, somewhere, that I have got to find, if Tip can show me where he is. Come, Tip ! "

" Oh, Jack ! You will not go without "— Jack turned his back to the door, and held out his arms. Esmée cast herself into them, and he kissed her in bitter silence, and went out.

These two were seated together again by the fire in the same room. It was four o'clock in the morning, but as dark as midnight. The floor in spots was wet with melted snow. They spoke seldom, in low, tired voices; it was generally Esmée who spoke. They had not been weeping, but their faces were changed and grown old. Jack shivered, and kept feeding the fire. On the bed in the adjoining room, cold as the snow in a deserted nest, lay their first guest, whom no house fire would ever warm.

"I cannot believe it. I cannot take it in. Are you sure there is nothing more we could do that a doctor would do if we had one?"

"We have done everything. It was too late when I found him."

"How is it possible? I have heard of persons lost for days — and this was only such a few hours."

"A few hours! Good God, Esmée! Come out with me, and stand five minutes in this storm, if you can. And he had been on snow-shoes all day; he had come all the way up-hill from town. He had had no rest, and nothing to eat. And then to turn about, and take it worse than ever!"

"It is an impossible thing," she reiterated. "I am crazy when I think of it."

Tip lifted his head uneasily, rose, and

tapped about the room, his long-nailed toes
rattling on the uncarpeted floor. He
paused, and licked up one of the pools of
melted snow. "Stop that!" Jack commanded. There was dead silence. Then
Tip began again his restless march about
the room, pausing at the bedroom door to
whine his questioning distress.

"Can't you make him stay in the
kitchen?" Esmée suggested timidly.

"It is cold in the kitchen. Tip has
earned his place by my fire as long as I
shall have one," said Jack, emphatically.

Down fell some crashing object, and was
shivered on the floor. The dog sprang up,
and howled; Esmée trembled like a leaf.

"It's only your little looking-glass," she
whispered. There was no mystery in its
having fallen in such a wind from the pro-
jecting log where Esmée, with more confidence than judgment, had propped it.

In silence both recalled the light words that
had passed when Jack had taken it down
from its high nail, saying that the mirrors
in his establishment had not been hung
with reference to persons of her size; and
Esmée could see the picture they had made,

putting their heads together before it, Jack stooping, with his hands on her shoulders, to bring his face in line with hers. Those laughing faces! All smiles, all tremulous mirth in that house had vanished as the reflections in a shattered mirror.

Jack got up, and fetched a broom, and swept the clinking fragments into the fire. The frame he broke in two and tossed after them.

"Call me as soon as it is light enough to start," he said to Esmée.

"But not unless it has stopped snowing?"

"Call me as soon as it is light, please," Jack repeated. He stumbled as he walked, like an old man. Esmée followed him into the drear little kitchen, where a single candle on the table was guttering in the draft. The windows were blank with frost, the boards cracked with the cold. Esmée helped prepare him a bed on a rude bunk against the wall, and Jack threw himself down on his pallet, and closed his eyes, without speaking. Esmée stood watching him in silence a moment; then she fell on her knees beside him on the floor.

"Say that you can forgive me! How shall I bear it all alone!"

At first Jack made no answer; he could not speak; his breath came deep and hard. Then he rose on one elbow, and looked at her with great stern eyes.

"Have I accused you? You did not do it. I did not do it. It happened — to show us what we are. We have broken with all the ties of family. We can have no brother or sister — our brothers and sisters are the rebels like ourselves; every man and woman whom society has branded and cast out. Sooner or later we shall embrace them all. Nothing healthy can come near us and not take harm from us. We are contamination to women and destruction to men. Poor Sid had better have come to a den of thieves and murderers than to his own brother's house last night; yet we might have done him worse harm if we had let him in. Now he is only dead — clean and true, as he lived. He is dead through my sin. Do you see, now, what this means to me?"

"I see," said Esmée, rising from her knees. She went out of the room, closing the door gently between them.

Jack lay stretching his aching muscles in one position after another, and every way he turned his thoughts pursued him. The brutality of his speech to Esmée wrought its anguish equally upon him, now that it was too late to get back a single word. Still, she must understand, — she would understand, when she came to think — how broken up he was in mind and body, how crazed for want of rest after that horrible night's work. This feeling of irresponsibility to himself satisfied him that she could not hold him responsible for his words at such a time. The strain he was supporting, mentally and physically, must absolve him if she had any consideration for him left.

So at length he slept. Esmée was careful not to disturb him. She had no need of bodily rest, and the beating of her heart and the ceaseless thinking went on and on.

"I am to be left here alone with *it*" — she glanced toward the room where the body lay — "while he goes for help to take it to town. He has not asked me if I can go through with this. If I should say to him, 'Spare me this awful trial,' he would answer, — and of course he would be right,

— ' There are only us two ; one to go and one to stay. Is it so much to ask of you after what has happened ? '

" He does not ask it ; he expects it. He is not my tender, remorseful lover now, dreading for me, every day, what his happiness must cost me. He is counting what I have cost him in other possessions which he might have had if he had not paid too great a price for one."

So these two had come to judge each other in the common misery that drove them apart. Toward daylight the snow ceased and the wind went down. Jack had forgotten to provide wood for Esmée's fire ; the room was growing cold, and the wood supply was in the kitchen, where he slept. She sat still and suffered mutely, rather than waken him before the time. This was not altogether consideration for him. It was partly wounded pride, inflicting its own suffering on the flesh after a moral scourging, either through one's own or another's conscience.

When the late morning slowly dawned, she went to waken him, obedient to orders. She made every effort to arouse him, but in vain. His sleep was like a trance. She had heard of cases of extreme mental and physical strain where a sleep like this, bordering on unconsciousness, had been nature's cure. She let him sleep.

Seeing that her movements did not disturb him, she went cautiously about the room, trying, now in forlorn sincerity, to adapt herself to the necessities of the situation. She did her best to make ready something in the nature of a breakfast for Jack when he should at length awaken. It promised to be a poor substitute, but the effort did her good.

It was after noon before Jack came to himself. He had been awake some little time, watching her, before she was aware of it. He could see for himself what she had been trying to accomplish, and he was greatly touched.

" Poor child ! " he said, and held out his arms.

She remained at a distance, slightly smiling, her eyes on the floor.

He did not press the moment of reconciliation. He got upon his feet, and, in the soldierly fashion of men who live in camps

and narrow quarters, began to fold his
blankets, and straighten things in his corner
of the room.

"If you will go into the sitting-room, I
will bring in the breakfast, such as it is,"
said Esmée. Jack obeyed her meekly.
The sitting-room fire had been relighted,
and was burning brightly. It was strange
to him to sit and see her wait upon him.
Stranger still was her silence. Here was a
new distress. He tried to pretend unconsciousness of the change in her.

"It is two o'clock," he said, looking at
his watch. "I'm afraid I shall be late getting back; but you must not worry. The
storm is over, and I know every foot of the
way."

"Did I do wrong," Esmée questioned
nervously, "not to call you? I tried very
hard, but you could not wake. You must
have needed to sleep, I think."

"Do you expect me to scold you every
time I speak, Esmée? I have said enough,
I think. Come here, dear girl. *I* need to
be forgiven now. It cuts me to the heart
to see you so humble. May God humble
me for those words I said!"

" You spoke the truth. Only we had not been telling each other the truth before."

"No. And we must stop it. We shall learn the truth fast enough. We need not make whips of it to lash each other with. Come here."

" I can't," said Esmée in a choking whisper.

" Yes, you can. You shall forgive me."

She shook her head. "That is not the question. You did not do it. I did not do it. God has done it — as you said."

" Did I say that? Did I presume to preach to you?"

" If I have done what you say — if I have cut you off from all human relations, and made your house worse than a den of thieves and murderers, how can anything be too bad for me to hear? What does it matter from whom I hear it?"

" I was beside myself. I was drunk with sorrow and fatigue."

" That is when people speak the truth, they say. I don't blame you, Jack. How should I? But you know it can never be the same, after this, with you or with me."

" Esmée," said Jack, after a long and

bitter silence, holding out his shaking hand,
" will you come with me in there, and look
at him? He knows the truth — the whole
truth. If you can see in his face anything
like scorn or reproach, anything but peace,
— peace beyond all conception, — then I
will agree that we part this day, forever.
Will you come?"

" Oh, Jack, you *are* beside yourself, now.
Do you think that I would go in there, in
the presence of *that* peace, and call on it for
my justification, and begin this thing again?
I should expect that peace would come to
me — the peace of instant death — for such
awful presumption."

" I did n't mean that — not to excuse
ourselves; only to bring back the trust that
was between us. Does this bitterness cure
the past? Have we not hurt each other
enough already?"

" I think so. It is sufficient for me.
But men, they say, get over such things,
and their lives go on, and they take their
places as before. I want you to " —

" There is nothing for me — will you
believe it? — more than there is for you.
Will you not do me that much justice, not

to treat this one passion of my life as —
what shall I say? It is not possible that
you can think such things. We must make
up to each other for what we have each cost
the other. Come. Let us go and stand
beside him — you and I, before the others
get here. It will do us good. Then we
will follow him out, on his way home, as far
as we can; and if there is any one in town
who has an account with me, he can settle
it there and then. Perhaps my mother will
have both her sons shipped home to her on
the same train."

Jack had not miscounted on the effect of
these words. They broke down Esmée's
purer resolution with their human appeal.
Yet he was not altogether selfish.

He held out his hand to her. She took
it, and they went together, shrinkingly, into
the presence of the dead. When they came
out, the eyes of both were wet.

Late as it was, it was inevitable that
Jack must start. Esmée watched him prepare once more for the journey. When he
was ready to set out, she said to him, with
an extreme effort:

"If any one should come while you are
gone, I am to let him in?"

" Do as you think best, dear ; but I am afraid that no one will disturb you. It will be a lonely watch. I wish I could help you through with it."

" It is my watch," said Esmée. " I must keep it."

She would have been thankful for the company even of Tip, to answer for something living, if not human, in the house ; but the dog insisted so savagely on following his master that she was forced to set him free. She closed the door after him, and locked it mechanically, hardly aware of what she did.

There is a growth of the spirit which is gradual, progressive, healthful, and therefore permanent. There are other psychical births that are forced, convulsive, agonizing in their suddenness. They may be premature, brought on by the shock of a great sorrow, or a sin perhaps committed without full knowledge of its nature, or realization of its consequences. Such births are perilous and unsure. Of these was the spiritual crisis through which Esmée was now passing.

She had made her choice : human love

was satisfied according to the natural law.
Now, in the hours of her solitary watch,
that irrevocable choice confronted her. It
was as a cup of trembling held to her lips
by the mystery of the Invisible, which says :
Whoever will drink of this cup of his desire,
be it soon, be it late, shall drain it to the
dregs, and " wring them out."   Esmée had
come very soon to the dregs of her cup of
trembling.

In such anguish and abasement her new
life of the spirit began. Will she have
strength to sustain it, or must it pass like a
shaken light into the keeping of a steadier
hand ?

She was but dimly aware of outward
changes as the ordeal wore on. It had been
pale daylight in the cabin, and now it was
dusk. It had been as still as death outside
after the night of storm, the cold relenting,
the frost trickling like tears down the pane ;
but now there was a rising stir. The soft,
wild gale, the chinook of the Northwest,
came roaring up the peak — the breath of
May, but the voice of March. The forest
began to murmur and moan, and strip its
white boughs of their burden, and all its

fairy frost-work melted like a dream. At intervals in the deep timber a strange sound was heard, the rush and thump of some soft, heavy mass into the snow. Esmée had never heard the sound before; it filled her with a creeping dread. Every separate distinct pounce — they came at intervals, near or far, but with no regularity — was a shock to her overwrought nerves. These sounds had taken sole possession of her ear. It was hence a double shock, at about the same hour of early twilight when her visitor had come the night before, to hear again a man's feet in the trench outside, and again a loud knock upon the door.

Her heart with its panting answered in her breast. There was a pause while outside the knocker seemed to listen, as he had done before. Then the new-born will of the woman fearfully took command of her cowering senses. Something that was beyond herself forced her to the door. Pale, and weak in every limb, she dragged herself to meet whatever it was that summoned her. This time she opened the door.

There stood a mild-faced man, in the dress of a miner, smiling apologetically. Esmée simply stared at him, and held the door wide. The man stepped hesitatingly inside, taking off his hat to the pale girl who looked at him so strangely.

David Bruce modestly attempted to give an incidental character to his visit by inventing an errand in that neighborhood.

" Excuse me, ma'am," he said. " I was going along over to the Mule Deer, but I thought I'd just ask if Mr. Waring's brother got through all right yesterday evenin'. It was so ugly outside."

The girl parted her lips to speak, but no sound came. The light shone in her ashy face. Her eyes were losing their expression. Bruce saw that she was fainting, and caught her as she fell.

The interview begun in this unpromising manner proved of the utmost comfort to Esmée. There was nothing in Bruce's manner to herself, nothing in his references to Jack, that implied any curiosity on his part as to the relation between them, or the least surprise at their being together at the Dreadnaught. He had " spared the situation " with an instinct that does not come from knowledge of the world.

He listened to her story of the night's tragedy, which she told with helpless severity, almost with indifference, as if it had happened to another.

He appeared to be greatly moved by it personally; its moral significance he did not seem to see. He sat helplessly repeating himself, in his efforts to give words to his sorrow for the "kid." His vocabulary being limited, and chiefly composed of words which he could not use before a lady, he was put to great inconvenience to do justice to his feelings.

He blamed himself and his brother for letting the young man go by their cabin on such a threatening day.

"Why, Jim and me we could n't get to sleep for thinkin' about him, 't was blowin' such a blizzard. Seemed like we could hear him a-yellin' to us, 'Is this the way to the Dreadnaught mine?' Wisht the Lord we 'd 'a' said it wa'n't. Well, sir, we don't want no more such foolishness. And that's partly why I come. We never thought but what he *had* got through, for all we was pestered about it, or else me and Jim would 'a' turned out last night. But what we was a-sayin' this morning was this: Them folks up there ain't acquainted with this country like we be — not in the winter-time. This here is what we call snow-slide weather. Hain't you been hearing how things is lettin' go? The snow slumpin' off the trees — you must have heard that. It 's lettin' go up above us, too. There 's a million ton of snow up there a-settlin' and a-crawlin' in this chinook, just a-gettin' ready to start to slide. We fellers in the mountains know how 't is. This cabin has stood all right so far, but the woods above was cut last summer. Now, I want you to come along with me right now. I 've got a handsleigh here. You can tuck yourself up on it, and we 'll pull out for the Mule Deer, and likely meet with Mr. Waring on the way. And if there 's a snow-slide here before morning, it 'll bury the dead, and not the living and the dead."

At these words the blood rushed to Esmée's cheek, and then dropped back to her heart, leaving her as white as snow.

" I don't remember that I have ever seen you before," she said; " but I thank you more than I ever thanked anybody in all my life."

David Bruce thought of course that she was going with him. But that was not what she meant. Her face shone. God, in his great mercy, had given her this one opportunity.

"This is my watch, you know. I cannot leave this house. But I don't think there will be a snow-slide. Things do not happen so simply as that. You don't know what I mean? But think a moment. You know, do you not, who I am? Should you think really that death is a thing that any friend of mine would wish to save me from? Life is what I am afraid of — long life to the end. I don't think there will be a snow-slide, not in time for me. But I thank you so much. You have made me feel so human — so like other people. You don't understand that, either? Well, no matter. I am just as grateful. I shall remember your visit all my life; and even if I live long, I doubt if I shall ever have a kinder visitor. I am much better for your coming, though you may think you have come for nothing. Now you must go before it gets too dark. You will go to the Mule Deer, will you not, and carry this same message to — there?"

" I 'm goin' to stop right here till Jack
Waring gets back."

" Oh, no, you 're not. You are going
this instant." She rose, and held out her
hand. She had that power over him that
one so much in earnest as she will always
have over one who is amazed and in doubt.

" Won't you shake hands with me ? "
Her thrilling voice made a sort of music of
the common words.

He took her hand, and wagged it clumsily
in a dazed way, and she almost pushed him
out of the house.

" Well, I 'll be hanged if that ain't the
meanest trick since I was born — to leave a
little lone woman watchin' with a dead man
in a cabin, with snow-slides startin' all over
the mountains ! What 's the matter with
me, anyhow ? Seem to be knocked silly
with her blamed queer talk. Heap of sense
in it, too. Would n't think one of her kind
would see it that way, though. Durned if I
know which kind she is. B'lieve I 'll go
back now. Why, Lord ! I must go back !
What 'll I say to Jim ? "

David Bruce had gained the top of the road

leading away from the mine before he came
to himself in a burst of unconscious profanity. He could hear the howling of the wind
around the horn of the peak. He looked up
and down, and considered a second.

In another second it was too late — too
late to add his life to hers, that instant buried beneath the avalanche.

A stroke out of a clear sky; a roar that
filled the air; a burst of light snow mounting over the tree-tops like steam condensed
above a rushing train; a concussion of wind
that felled trees in the valley a hundred
yards from the spot where the plunging mass
shot down — then the chinook eddied back,
across the track of the snow-slide, and went
storming up the peak.

TRAVELING BUTTES is a lone stage-station on the road, largely speaking, from Blackfoot to Boise. I do not know whether the stages take that road now, but ten years ago they did, and the man who kept the stage-house was a person of primitive habits and corresponding appearance named Gilroy.

The stage-house is perhaps half a mile from the foot of the largest butte, one of three that loom on the horizon, and appear to " travel " from you, as you approach them from the plains. A day's ride with the Buttes as a landmark is like a stern chase, in that you seem never to gain upon them.

From the stage-house the plain slopes up to the foot of the Big Butte, which rises suddenly in the form of an enormous tepee, as if Gitche Manito, the mighty, had here descended and pitched his tent for a council of the nations.

The country is destitute of water. To say

that it is "thirsty" is to mock with vain imagery that dead and mummied land on the borders of the Black Lava. The people at the stage-house had located a precious spring, four miles up, in a cleft near the top of the Big Butte; they piped the water down to the house and they sold it to travelers on that Jericho road at so much per horse. The man was thrown in, but the man usually drank whisky.

Our guide commented unfavorably on this species of husbandry, which is common enough in the arid West, and as legitimate as selling oats or hay; but he chose to resent it in the case of Gilroy, and to look upon it as an instance of individual and exceptional meanness.

"Any man that will jump God's water in a place like this, and sell it the same as drinks — he'd sell water to his own father in hell!"

This was our guide's opinion of Gilroy. He was equally frank, and much more explicit, in regard to Gilroy's sons. "But," he concluded, with a philosopher's acceptance of existing facts, "it ain't likely that any of that outfit will ever git into trouble, so long as Maverick is sheriff of Lemhi County."

We were about to ask why, when we drove up to the stage-house, and Maverick himself stepped out and took our horses.

"What the — infernal has happened to the man?" my companion, Ferris, exclaimed; and our guide answered indifferently, as if he were speaking of the weather, —

"Some Injuns caught him alone in an out-o'-the-way ranch, when he was a kid, and took a notion to play with him. This is what was left when they got through. I never see but one worse-looking man," he added, speaking low, as Maverick passed us with the team : " him a bear wiped over the head with its paw. 'T was quicker over with, I expect, but he lived, and *he* looked worse than Maverick."

"Then I hope to the Lord I may never see him!" Ferris ejaculated; and I noticed that he left his dinner untasted, though he had boasted of a hunter's appetite.

We were two college friends on a hunting trip, but we had not got into the country of game. In two days more we expected to make Jackson's Hole, and I may mention that "hole," in this region, signifies any small, deep valley, well hidden amidst high

mountains, where moisture is perennial, and
grass abounds. In these pockets of plenty,
herds of elk gather and feed as tame as park
pets; and other hunted creatures, as wild but
less innocent, often find sanctuary here, and
cache their stolen stock and other spoil of
the road and the range.

We did not forget to put our question concerning Maverick, that unhappy man, in his
character of legalized protector of the Gilroy
gang. What did our free-spoken guide mean
by that insinuation?

We were told that Gilroy, in his rough-
handed way, had been as a father to the lad,
after the savages wreaked their pleasure on
him: and his people being dead or scattered,
Maverick had made himself useful in various
humble capacities at the stage-house, and had
finally become a sort of factotum there and
a member of the family. And though perfectly square himself, and much respected on
account of his personal courage and singular
misfortunes, he could never see the old man's
crookedness, nor the more than crookedness
of his sons. He was like a son of the house,
himself; but most persons agreed that it was
not as a brother he felt toward Rose Gilroy.

And a tough lookout it was for the girl; for Maverick was one whom no man would lightly cross, and in her case he was acting as "general dog around the place," as our guide called it. The young fellows were shy of the house, notwithstanding the attraction it held. It was likely to be Maverick or nobody for Rose.

We did not see Rose Gilroy, but we heard her step in the stage-house kitchen, and her voice, as clear as a lark's, giving orders to the tall, stooping, fair young Swede, who waited on us at table, and did other work of a menial character in that singular establishment.

"How is it the watch-dog allows such a pretty sprig as that around the place?" Ferris questioned, eying our knight of the trencher, who blushed to feel himself remarked.

"He won't stay," our guide pronounced; "they don't none of 'em stay when they 're good-lookin'. The old man he 's failin' considerable these days, — gettin' kind o' silly, — and the boys are away the heft of the time. Maverick pretty much runs the place. I don't justly blame the critter. He 's

watched that little Rose grow up from a
baby. How 's he goin' to quit being fond of
her now she 's a woman ? I dare say he 'd a
heap sooner she 'd stayed a little girl. And
these yere boys around here they 're a triflin'
set, not half so able to take care of her as
Maverick. He 's got the sense and he 's got
the sand ; but there 's that awful head on
him ! I don't blame him much, lookin' the
way he does, and feelin' the same as any
other man."

We left Traveling Buttes and its cruel
little love-story, but we had not gone a mile
when a horseman overtook us with a message for Ferris from his new foreman at the
ranch, a summons which called him back for
a day at the least. Ferris was exceedingly
annoyed: a day at the ranch meant four
days on the road; but the business was imperative. We held a brief council, and decided that, with Ferris returning, our guide
should push on with the animals and camp
outfit into a country of grass, and look up a
good camping-spot (which might not be the
first place he struck) this side of Jackson's
Hole. It remained for me to choose between going with the stuff, or staying for a

longer look at the phenomenal Black Lava fields at Arco ; Arco being another name for desolation on the very edge of that weird stone sea. This was my ostensible reason for choosing to remain at Arco ; but I will not say the reflection did not cross me that Arco is only sixteen miles from Traveling Buttes — not an insurmountable distance between geology and a pretty girl, when one is five and twenty, and has not seen a pretty face for a month of Sundays.

Arco, at that time, consisted of the stage-house, a store, and one or two cabins — a poor little seed of civilization dropped by the wayside, between the Black Lava and the hills where Lost River comes down and "sinks" on the edge of the lava. The station is somewhat back from the road, with its face — a very grimy, unwashed countenance — to the lava. Quaking asps and mountain birches follow the water, pausing a little way up the gulch behind the house, but the eager grass tracks it all the way till it vanishes ; and the dry bed of the stream goes on and spreads in a mass of coarse sand and gravel, beaten flat, flailed by the feet of countless driven sheep that have gathered here. For this road is on the great overland sheep-trail from Oregon eastward — the march of the million mouths, and what the mouths do not devour the feet tramp down.

The staple topic of conversation at Arco was one very common in the far west, when a tenderfoot is of the company. The poorest place can boast of some distinction, and Arco, though hardly on the highroad of fashion and commerce, had frequently been named in print in connection with crime of a highly sensational and picturesque character. Scarcely another fifty miles of stage-road could boast of so many and such successful road-jobs; and although these affairs were of almost monthly occurrence, and might be looked for to come off always within that noted danger-limit, yet it was a fact that the law had never yet laid finger on a man of the gang, nor gained the smallest clew to their hide-out. It was a difficult country around Arco, one that lent itself to secrecy. The road-agents came, and took, and vanished as if the hills were their co-partners as well as the receivers of their goods. As for the lava, which was its front dooryard, so to speak, for a hundred miles, the man did not live who could say he had crossed it. What it held or was capable of hiding, in life or in death, no man knew.

The day after Ferris left me I rode out upon that arrested tide — those silent breakers which for ages have threatened, but never reached, the shore. I tried to fancy it as it must once have been, a sluggish, vitreous flood, filling the great valley, and stiffening as it slowly pushed toward the bases of the hills. It climbed and spread, as dough rises and crawls over the edge of the pan. The Black Lava is always called a sea — that image is inevitable; yet its movement had never in the least the character of water. " This is where hell pops," an old plainsman feelingly described it, and the suggestion is perfect. The colors of the rock are those produced by fire : its texture is that of slag from a furnace. One sees how the lava hardened into a crust, which cracked and sank in places, mingling its tumbled edges with the creeping flood not cooled beneath. After all movement had ceased and the mass was still, time began upon its tortured configurations, crumbled and wore and broke, and sifted a little earth here and there, and sealed the burnt rock with fairy print of lichens, serpent-green and orange and rust-red. The spring rains left shallow pools which the summer dried. Across it, a few dim trails wander a little way and give out, like the water.

For a hundred miles to the Snake River this Plutonian gulf obliterates the land — holds it against occupation or travel. The shoes of a marching army would be cut from their feet before they had gone a dozen miles across it; horses would have no feet left; and water would have to be packed as on an ocean, or a desert, cruise.

I rode over places where the rock rang beneath my horse's hoofs like the iron cover of a manhole. I followed the hollow ridges that mounted often forty feet above my head, but always with that gruesome effect of thickening movement — that sluggish, atomic crawl; and I thought how one man pursuing another into this frozen hell might lose himself, but never find the object of his quest. If he took the wrong furrow, he could not cross from one blind gut into another, nor hope to meet the fugitive at any future turning.

I don't know why the fancy of a flight and pursuit should so have haunted me, in connection with the Black Lava; probably the desperate and lawless character of our conversation at the stage-house gave rise to it.

I had fallen completely under the spell of that skeleton flood. I watched the sun sink, as it sinks at sea, beyond its utmost ragged ridges; I sat on the borders of it, and stared across it in the gray moonlight; I rode out upon it when the Buttes, in their delusive nearness, were as blue as the gates of amethyst, and the morning was as fair as one great pearl; but no peace or radiance of heaven or earth could change its aspect more than that of a mound of skulls. When I began to dream about it, I thought I must be getting morbid. This is worse than Gilroy's, I said; and I promised myself I would ride up there next day and see if by chance one might get a peep at the Rose that all were praising, but none dared put forth a hand to pluck. Was it indeed so hard a case for the Rose? There are women who can love a man for the perils he has passed. Alas, Maverick! could any one get used to a face like that?

Here, surely, was the story of Beauty and
her poor Beast humbly awaiting, in the mask
of a brutish deformity, the recognition of
Love pure enough to divine the soul beneath,
and unselfish enough to deliver it. Was
there such love as that at Gilroy's? However, I did not make that ride.

It was the fourth night of clear, desert
moonlight since Ferris had left me: I was
sleepless, and so I heard the first faint throb
of a horse's feet approaching from the east,
coming on at a great pace, and making the
turn to the stage-house. I looked out, and
on the trodden space in front I saw Maverick dismounting from a badly blown horse.

"Halloo! what's up?" I called from the
open window of my bedroom on the ground-
floor.

"Did two men pass here on horseback
since dark?"

"Yes," I said; "about twelve o'clock: a
tall man and a little short fellow."

"Did they stop to water?"

"No, they did not; and they seemed in
such a tearing hurry that I watched them
down the road" —

"I am after those men, and I want a fresh horse," he cut in. "Call up somebody quick!"

"Shall you take one of the boys along?" I inquired, with half an eye to myself, after I had obeyed his command.

He shook his head. "Only one horse here that's good for anything: I want that myself."

"There is my horse," I suggested; "but I'd rather be the one who rides her. She belongs to a friend."

"Take her, and come on, then, but understand — this ain't a Sunday-school picnic."

"I'm with you, if you'll have me."

"I'd sooner have your horse," he remarked, shifting the quid of tobacco in his cheek.

"You can't have her without me, unless you steal her," I said.

"Git your gun, then, and shove some grub into your pockets: I can't wait for nobody."

He swung himself into the saddle.

"What road do you take?"

"There ain't but one," he shouted, and pointed straight ahead.

I overtook him easily within the hour; he

was saving his horse, for this was his last chance to change until Champagne Station, fifty miles away.

He gave me rather a cynical smile of recognition as I ranged alongside, as if to say, "You 'll probably get enough of this before we are through." The horses settled down to their work, and they "humped theirselves," as Maverick put it, in the cool hours before sunrise.

At daybreak his awful face struck me all afresh, as inscrutable in its strange distortion as some stone god in the desert, from whose graven hideousness a thousand years of mornings have silently drawn the veil.

"What do you want those fellows for?" I asked, as we rode. I had taken for granted that we were hunting suspects of the road-agent persuasion.

"I want 'em on general principles," he answered shortly.

"Do you think you know them?"

"I think they 'll know me. All depends on how they act when we get within range. If they don't pay no attention to us, we 'll send a shot across their bows. But more likely they 'll speak first."

He was very gloomy, and would keep silence for an hour at a time. Once he turned on me as with a sudden misgiving.

"See here, don't you git excited; and whatever happens, don't you meddle with the little one. If the big fellow cuts up rough, he'll take his chances, but you leave the little one to me. I want him — I want him for State's evidence," he finished hoarsely.

"The little one must be the Benjamin of the family," I thought — "one of the bad young Gilroys, whose time has come at last; and sheriff Maverick finds his duty hard."

I could not say whether I really wished the men to be overtaken, but the spirit of the chase had undoubtedly entered into my blood. I felt as most men do, who are not saints or cowards, when such work as this is to be done. But I knew I had no business to be along. It was one thing for Maverick, but the part of an amateur in a man-hunt is not one to boast of.

The sun was now high, and the fresh tracks ahead of us were plain in the dust. Once they left the road and strayed off into the lava, incomprehensibly to me; but

Maverick understood, and pressed forward. "We'll strike them again further on. D—— fool!" he muttered, and I observed that he alluded but to one, "huntin' water-holes in the lava in the tail end of August!"

They could not have found water, for at Belgian Flat they had stopped and dug for it in the gravel, where a little stream in freshet time comes down the gulch from the snow-fields higher up, and sinks, as at Arco, on the lip of the lava. They had dug, and found it, and saved us the trouble, as Maverick remarked.

Considerable water had gathered since the flight had paused here and lost precious time. We drank our fill, refreshed our horses, and shifted the saddle-girths; and I managed to stow away my lunch during the next mile or so, after offering to share it with Maverick, who refused it as if the notion of food made him sick. He had considerable whisky aboard, but he was, I judged, one of those men on whom drink has little effect; else some counter-flame of excitement was fighting it in his blood.

I looked for the development of the personal complication whenever we should come up with the chase, for the man's eye burned, and had his branded countenance been capable of any expression that was not cruelly travestied, he would have looked the impersonation of wild justice.

It was now high noon, and our horses were beginning to feel the steady work; yet we had not ridden as they brought the good news from Ghent: that is the pace of a great lyric; but it's not the pace at which justice, or even vengeance, travels in the far West. Even the furies take it coolly when they pursue a man over these roads, and on these poor brutes of horses, in fifty-mile stages, with drought thrown in.

Maverick had had no mercy on the pony that brought him sixteen miles; but this piece of horse-flesh he now bestrode must last him through at least to Champagne Station, should we not overhaul our men before. He knew well when to press and when to spare the pace, a species of purely practical consideration which seemed habitual with him; he rode like an automaton, his baleful face borne straight before him — the Gorgon's head.

Beyond Belgian Flat — how far beyond

I do not remember, for I was beginning to feel the work, too, and the country looked all alike to me as we made it, mile by mile — the road follows close along by the lava, but the hills recede, and a little trail cuts across, meeting the road again at Deadman's Flat. Here we could not trust to the track, which from the nature of the ground was indistinct. So we divided our forces, Maverick taking the trail, — which I was quite willing he should do, for it had a look of most sinister invitation, — while I continued by the longer road. Our little discussion, or some atmospheric change, — some breath of coolness from the hills, — had brought me up out of my stupor of weariness. I began to feel both alert and nervous ; my heart was beating fast. The still sunshine lay all around us, but where Maverick's white horse was climbing, the shadows were turning eastward, and the deep gulches, with their patches of aspen, were purple instead of brown. The aspens were left shaking where he broke through them and passed out of sight.

I kept on at a good pace, and about three o'clock I, being then as much as half a mile away, saw the spot which I knew must be Deadman's Flat; and there were our men, the tall one and his boyish mate, standing quietly by their horses in broad sunlight, as if there were no one within a hundred miles. Their horses had drunk, and were cropping the thin grass, which had set its tooth in the gravel where, as at the other places, a living stream had perished. I spurred forward, with my heart thumping, but before they saw me I saw Maverick coming down the little gulch; and from the way he came I knew that he had seen them.

The scene was awful in its treacherous peacefulness. Their shadows slept on the broad bed of sunlight, and the gulch was as cool and still as a lady's chamber. The great dead desert received the silence like a secret.

Tenderfoot as I was, I knew quite well what must happen now; yet I was not prepared — could not realize it — even when the tall one put his hand quickly behind him and stepped ahead of his horse. There was the flash of his pistol, and the loud crack echoing in the hill; a second shot, and then Maverick replied deliberately, and the tall one was down, with his face in the grass.

I heard a scream that sounded strangely like a woman's ; but there were only the three, the little one, acting wildly, and Maverick bending over him who lay with his face in the grass. I saw him turn the body over, and the little fellow seemed to protest, and to try to push him away. I thought it strange he made no more of a fight, but I was not near enough to hear what those two said to each other.

Still, the tragedy did not come home to me. It was all like a scene, and I was without feeling in it except for that nervous trembling which I could not control.

Maverick stood up at length, and came slowly toward me, wiping his face. He kept his hat in his hand, and, looking down at it, said huskily : —

" I gave that man his life when I found him last spring runnin' loose like a wild thing in the mountains, and now I 've took it ; and God above knows I had no grudge ag'in' him, if he had stayed in his place. But he would have it so."

" Maverick, I saw it all, and I can swear it was self-defense."

His face drew into the tortured grimace which was his smile. " This here will never come before a jury," he said. " It 's a family affair. Did ye see how he acted ? Steppin' up to me like he was a first-class shot, or else a fool. He ain't nary one; he 's a poor silly tool, the whip-hand of a girl that 's boltin' from her friends like they was her mortal enemies. Go and take a look at him ; then maybe you 'll understand."

He paused, and uttered the name of Jesus Christ, but not as such men often use it, with an inconsequence dreadful to hear : he was not idly swearing, but calling that name to witness solemnly in a case that would never come before a jury.

I began to understand.

" Is it — is the girl " —

" Yes; it 's our poor little Rose — that 's the little one, in the gray hat. She 'll give herself away if I don't. She don't care for nothin' nor nobody. She was runnin' away with that fellow — that dish-washin' Swede what I found in the mountings eatin' roots like a ground-hog, with the ends of his feet

froze off. Now you know all I know — and
more than she knows, for she thinks she
was fond of him. She wa'n't, never — for I
watched 'em, and I know. She was crazy to
git away, and she took him for the chance."

His excitement passed, and we sat apart
and watched the pair at a distance. She —
the little one — sat as passively by her dead
as Maverick pondering his cruel deed; but
with both it was a hopeless quiet.

" Come," he said at length, " I 've got to
bury him. You look after her, and keep
her with you till I git through. I 'm givin'
you the hardest part," he added wistfully,
as if he fully realized how he had cut himself
off from all such duties, henceforth, to the
girl he was consigning to a stranger's care.

I told him I thought that the funeral had
more need of me than the mourner, and I
shrank from intruding myself.

" I dassent leave her by herself — see?
I don't know what notion she may take next,
and she won't let me come within a rope's
len'th of her."

I will not go over again that miserable
hour in the willows, where I made her stay
with me, out of sight of what Maverick was

doing.   Ours were the tender mercies of the
wicked, I fear ; but she must have felt that
sympathy at least was near her, if not help.
I will not say that her youth and distressful
loveliness did not sharpen my perception of
a sweet life wasted, gone utterly astray, which
might have brought God's blessing into
some man's home — perhaps Maverick's,
had he not been so hardly dealt with.   She
was not of that great disposition of heart
which can love best that which has sorest
need of love ; but she was all woman, and
helpless and distraught with her tangle of
grief and despair, the nature of which I
could only half comprehend.

We sat there by the sunken stream, on
the hot gravel where the sun had lain, the
willows sifting their inconstant shadows over
us ; and I thought how other things as
precious as " God's water " go astray on the
Jericho road, or are captured and sold for a
price, while dry hearts ache with the thirst
that asks a " draught divine."

The man's felt hat she wore, pulled down
over her face, was pinned to her coil of
braids which had slipped from the crown of
her head.   The hat was no longer even a

protection; she cast it off, and the blond
braids, that had not been smoothed for a
day and night, fell like ropes down her back.
The sun had burned her cheeks and neck to
a clear crimson; her blue eyes were as wild
with weeping as a child's. She was a rose,
but a rose that had been trampled in the
dust; and her prayer was to be left there,
rather than that we should take her home.

I suppose I must have had some influence
over her, for she allowed me to help her to arrange her forlorn disguise, and put her on her
horse, which was more than could have been
expected from the way she had received me.
And so, about four o'clock, we started back.

There was a scene when we headed the
horses to the west; she protesting with wild
sobs that she would not, could not, go home,
that she would rather die, that we should
never get her back alive, and so on. Maverick stood aside bitterly, and left her to
me, and I was aware of a grotesque touch of
jealousy — which, after all, was perhaps
natural — in his dour face whenever he
looked back at us. He kept some distance
ahead, and waited for us when we fell too
far in the rear.

This would happen when from time to time her situation seemed to overpower her, and she would stop in the road, and wring her hands, and try to throw herself out of the saddle, and pray me to let her go.

"Go where?" I would ask. "Where do you wish to go? Have you any plan, or suggestion, that I could help you to carry out?" But I said it only to show her how hopeless her resistance was. This she would own piteously, and say: "Nobody can help me. There ain't nowhere for me to go. But I can't go back. You won't let him make me, will you?"

"Why cannot you go back to your father and your brothers?"

This would usually silence her, and, setting her teeth upon her trouble, she would ride on, while I reproached myself, I knew not why.

After one of these struggles — when she had given in to the force of circumstances, but still unconsenting and rebellious — Maverick fell back, and ranged his horse by her other side.

"I know partly what's troubling you, and I'd rid you of that part quick enough," he said, with a kind of dogged patience in his hard voice ; " but you can't get on there without me. You know that, don't you? You don't blame me for staying ? "

" I don't blame you for anything but what you've done to-day. You've broke my heart, and ruined me, and took away my last chance, and I don't care what becomes of me, so I don't have to go back."

" You don't have to any more than you have to live. Dyin' is a good deal easier, but we can't always die when we want to. Suppose I found a little lost child on the road, and it cried to go home, and I did n't know where ' home ' was, would I leave it there just because it cried and hung back? I'd take you to a better home if I knew of one; but I don't. And there's the old man. I suppose we could get some doctor to certify that he's out of his mind, and get him sent up to Blackfoot; but I guess we'd have to buy the doctor first."

" Oh, hush, do, and leave me alone," she said.

Maverick dug his spurs into his horse, and plunged ahead.

" There," she cried, " now you know part

of it; but it's the least part — the least, the least! Poor father, he's awful queer. He don't more than half the time know who I am," she whispered. "But it ain't him I'm running away from. It's myself—my own life."

"What is it — can't you tell me?"

She shook her head, but she kept on telling, as if she were talking to herself.

"Father he's like I told you, and the boys — oh, that's worse! I can't get a decent woman to come there and live, and the women at Arco won't speak to me because I'm livin' there alone. They say — they think I ought to get married — to Maverick or somebody. I'll die first. I *will* die, if there's any way to, before I'll marry him!"

This may not sound like tragedy as I tell it, but I think it was tragedy to her. I tried to persuade her that it must be her imagination about the women at Arco; or, if some of them did talk, — as indeed I myself had heard, to my shame and disgust, —I told her I had never known that place where there was not one woman, at least, who could understand and help another in her trouble.

"*I* don't know of any," she said simply.

There was no more to do but ride on, feeling like her executioner; but

> "Ride hooly, ride hooly, now, gentlemen,
> Ride hooly now wi' me,"

came into my mind; and no man ever kept beside a "wearier burd," on a sadder journey.

At dusk we came to Belgian Flat, and here Maverick, dismounting, mixed a little whisky in his flask with water which he dipped from the pool. She must have recalled who dug the well, and with whom she had drunk in the morning. He held it to her lips. She rejected it with a strong shudder of disgust.

"Drink it!" he commanded. "You'll kill yourself, carryin' on like this." He pressed it on her, but she turned away her face like a sick and rebellious child.

"Maybe she'll drink it for you," said Maverick, with bitter patience, handing me the cup.

"Will you?" I asked her gently. She shook her head, but at the same time she let me take her hand, and put it down from her face, and I held the cup to her lips.

She drank it, every drop. It made her deathly sick, and I took her off her horse, and made a pillow of my coat, so that she could lie down. In ten minutes she was asleep. Maverick covered her with his coat after she was no longer conscious.

We built a fire on the edge of the lava, for we were both chilled and both miserable, each for his own part in that day's work.

The flat is a little cup-shaped valley formed by high hills, like dark walls, shutting it in. The lava creeps up to it in front.

We hovered over the fire, and Maverick fed it, savagely, in silence. He did not recognize my presence by a word — not so much as if I had been a strange dog. I relieved him of it after a while, and went out a little way on the lava. At first all was blackness after the strong glare of the fire ; but gradually the desolation took shape, and I stumbled about in it, with my shadow mocking me in derisive beckonings, or crouching close at my heels, as the red flames towered or fell. I stayed out there till I was chilled to the bone, and then went back defiantly. Maverick sat as if he had not moved, his elbows on his knees, his face in his hands. I wondered if he were thinking of that other sleeper under the birches of Deadman's Gulch, victim of an unhappy girl's revolt. Had she loved him? Had she deceived him as well as herself? It seemed to me they were all like children who had lost their way home.

By midnight the moon had risen high enough to look at us coldly over the tops of the great hills. Their shadows crept forth upon the lava. The fire had died down. Maverick rose, and scattered the winking brands with his boot-heel.

"We must pull out," he said. "I'll saddle up, if you will" — The hoarseness in his voice choked him, and he nodded toward the sleeper.

I dreaded to waken the poor Rose. She was very meek and quiet after the brief respite sleep had given her. She sat quite still, and watched me while I shook the sand from my coat, put it on, and buttoned it to the chin, and drew my hat down more firmly. There was a kind of magnetism in her gaze; I felt it creep over me like the touch of a soft hand.

When her horse was ready, Maverick brought it, and left it standing near, and went back to his own, without looking toward us.

"Come, you poor, tired little girl," I said, holding out my hand. She could not find her way at first in the uncertain light, and she seemed half asleep still, so I kept her hand in mine, and guided her to her horse. "Now, once more up," I encouraged her; and suddenly she was clinging to me, and whispering passionately:

"Can't you take me somewhere? Where are those women that you know?" she cried, shaking from head to foot.

"Dear little soul, all the women I know are two thousand miles away," I answered.

"But can't you take me *somewhere?* There must be some place. I know you would be good to me; and you could go away afterward, and I would n't trouble you any more."

"My child, there is not a place under the heavens where I could take you. You must go on like a brave girl, and trust to your friends. Keep up your heart, and the way will open. God will not forget you," I

said, and may He forgive me for talking
cant to that poor soul in her bitter ex-
tremity.

She stood perfectly still one moment
while I held her by the hands. I think she
could have heard my heart beat; but there
was nothing I could do. Even now I wake
in the night, and wonder if there was any
other way — but one; the way that for one
wild moment I was half tempted to take.

" Yes ; the way will open," she said very
low. She cast off my hands, and in a
second she was in the saddle, and off up the
road, riding for her life. And we two men
knew no better than to follow her.

I knew better, or I think, now, that I
did. I told Maverick we had pushed her
far enough. I begged him to hold up and
at least not to let her see us on her track.
He never answered a word, but kept straight
on, as if possessed. I don't think he knew
what he was doing. At least there was only
one thing *he* was capable of doing — following that girl till he dropped.

Two miles beyond the Flat there is another turn, where the shoulder of a hill
comes down and crowds the road, which

passes out of sight. She saw us hard upon her, as she reached this bend. Maverick was ahead. Her horse was doing all he could, but it was plain he could not do much more. She looked back, and flung out her hand in the man's sleeve that half covered it. She gave a little whimpering cry, the most dreadful sound I ever heard from any hunted thing.

We made the turn after her; and there lay the road white in the moonlight, and as bare as my hand. She had escaped us.

We pulled up the horses, and listened. Not a sound came from the hills or the dark gulches, where the wind was stirring the quaking asps; the lonesome hush-sh made the silence deeper. But we heard a horse's step go clink, clinking — a loose, uncertain step wandering away in the lava.

"Look! look there! My God!" groaned Maverick.

There was her horse limping along one of the hollow ridges, but the saddle was empty.

"She has taken to the lava!"

I had no need to be told what that meant; but if I had needed, I learned what it meant before the night was through. I think that if I were a poet, I could add another "dolorous circle" to the wailing-place for lost souls.

But she had found a way. Somewhere in that stony-hearted wilderness she is at rest. We shall see her again when the sea — the stupid, cruel sea that crawls upon the land — gives up its dead.

ON A SIDE-TRACK

I

IT was the second week in February, but winter had taken a fresh hold: the stockmen were grumbling; freight was dull, and travel light on the white Northwestern lines. In the Portland car from Omaha there were but four passengers: father and daughter, — a gentle, unsophisticated pair, — and two strong-faced men, fellow-travelers also, keeping each other's company in a silent but close and conspicuous proximity. They shared the same section, the younger man sleeping above, going to bed before, and rising later than, his companion; and whenever he changed his seat or made an unexpected movement, the eyes of the elder man followed him, and they were never far from him at any time.

The elder was a plain farmer type of man, with a clean-shaven, straight upper lip, a grizzled beard covering the lower half of his

face, and humorous wrinkles spreading from
the corners of his keen gray eyes.

The younger showed in his striking person that union of good blood with hard conditions so often seen in the old-young grad-
uates of the life schools of the West. His
hands and face were dark with exposure to
the sun, not of parks and club-grounds and
seaside piazzas, but the dry untempered
light of the desert and the plains. His dark
eye was distinctively masculine, — if there
be such a thing as gender in features, —
bold, ardent, and possessive; but now it
was clouded with sadness that did not pass
like a mood, though he looked capable of
moods.

He was dressed in the demi-toilet which
answers for dinners in the West, on occa-
sions where a dress-coat is not required. In
itself the costume was correct, even fastid-
ious, in its details, but on board an overland train there was a foppish unsuitability
in it that "gave the wearer away," as another man would have said — put him at a
disadvantage, notwithstanding his splendid
physique, and the sad, rather fine preoccu-
pation of his manner. He looked like a

very real person dressed for a trifling part, which he lays aside between the scenes while he thinks about his sick child, or his debts, or his friend with whom he has quarreled.

But these incongruities, especially the one of dress, might easily have escaped a pair of eyes so confiding and unworldly as those of the young girl in the opposite section; they had escaped her, but not the incongruity of youth with so much sadness. The girl and her father had boarded the car at Omaha, escorted by the porter of one of the forward sleepers on the same train. They had come from farther East. The old gentleman appeared to be an invalid; but they gave little trouble. The porter had much leisure on his hands, which he bestowed in arrears of sleep on the end seat forward. The conductor made up his accounts in the empty drawing-room, or looked at himself in the mirrors, or stretched his legs on the velvet sofas. He was a young fellow, with a tendency to jokes and snatches of song and talk of a light character when not on duty. He talked sometimes with the porter in low tones, and then both looked at the pair of travelers in No. 8, and the younger man seemed moodily aware of their observation.

On the first morning out from Omaha the old gentleman kept his berth until nine or ten o'clock. At eight his daughter brought him a cup of chocolate and a sandwich, and sat between his curtains, chatting with him cozily. In speaking together they used the language of the Society of Friends.

The young man opposite listened attentively to the girl's voice; it was as sweet as the piping of birds at daybreak. Phebe her father called her.

Afterward Phebe sat in the empty section next her father's. The table before her was spread with a fresh napkin, and a few pieces of old household silver and china which she had taken from her lunch-basket.

She and her father were economical travelers, but in all their belongings there was the refinement of modest suitability and an exquisite cleanliness. Her own order for breakfast was confined to a cup of coffee, which the porter was preparing in the buffet-kitchen.

" Would you mind changing places with me ? "

The young man in No. 8 spoke to his companion, who sat opposite reading a newspaper. They changed seats, and by this arrangement the younger could look at Phebe, who innocently gave him every advantage to study her sober and delicate profile against the white snow-light, as she sat watching the dreary cattle-ranges of Wyoming swim past the car window.

Her hair had been brushed, and her face washed in the bitter alkaline waters of the plains, with the uncompromising severity of one whose standards of personal adornment are limited to the sternest ideals of neatness and purity. Yet her fair face bloomed, like a winter sunrise, with tints of rose and pearl and sapphire blue, and the pale gold of winter sunshine was in her satin-smooth hair.

The young man did not fail to include in his study of Phebe the modest breakfast equipment set out before her. He perfectly recalled the pattern of the white-and-gold china, the touch, the very taste, of the thin, bright old silver spoons; they were like his grandmother's tea-things in the family homestead in the country, where he had spent his summers as a boy. The look of them touched him nearly, but not happily, it would seem, from his expression.

The porter came with the cup of coffee, and offered a number of patronizing suggestions in the line of his service, which the young girl declined. She set forth a meek choice of food, blushing faintly in deprecation of the young man's eyes, of which she began to be aware. Evidently she was not yet hardened to the practice of eating in public.

He took the hint, and retired to his corner, opening a newspaper between himself and Phebe.

Presently he heard her call the porter in a small, ineffectual voice. The porter did not come. She waited a little, and called again, with no better result. He put down his newspaper.

" If you will press the button at your left," he suggested.

" The button ! " she repeated, looking at him helplessly.

He sprang to assist her. As he did so his companion flung down his paper, and jumped in front of him. The eyes of the two met. A hot flush rose to the young man's eyebrows.

"I am calling the porter for her."

"Oh!" said the other, and he sat down again; but he kept an eye upon the angry youth, who leaned across Phebe's seat, and touched the electric button.

"Little girl had n't got on to it, eh?" the grizzled man remarked pleasantly, when his companion had resumed his seat.

There was no answer.

"Nice folks; from the country, some-wheres back East, I should guess," the imperturbable one continued. "Old man seems sort of sickly. Making a move on account of his health, likely. Great mistake — old folks turning out in winter huntin' a climate."

The young man remained silent, and the elder returned to his paper.

At Cheyenne, where the train halts for dinner, the young girl helped her father into his outer garments, buttoned herself hastily into her homespun jacket bordered with gray fur, pinned her little hat firmly to her crown of golden braids, hid her hands in her muff, — she did not wait to put on gloves, — and led the way to the dining-room.

The travelers in No. 8 disposed of their meal rapidly, in their usual close but silent conjunction, and returned at once to the car.

The old gentleman and his daughter walked the windy platform, and cast rather forlorn glances at the crowd bustling about in the bleak winter sunlight. When they took their seats again, the father's pale blue eyes were still paler, his face looked white and drawn with the cold; but Phebe was like a rose: with her wonderful, pure color the girl was beautiful. The young man of No. 8 looked at her with a startled reluctance, as if her sweetness wounded him.

Then he seemed to have resolved to look at her no more. He leaned his head back in his corner, and closed his eyes; the train shook him slightly as he sat in moody pre-occupation with his thoughts, and the miles of track flew by.

At Green River, at midnight, the Portland car was dropped by its convoy of the Union Pacific, and was coupled with a train making up for the Oregon Short Line. There was hooting and backing of engines,

slamming of car doors, flashing of con-
ductors' lanterns, voices calling across the
tracks. One of these voices could be heard,
in the wakeful silence within the car, as an
engine from the west steamed past in the
glare of its snow-wreathed headlight.

"No. 10 stuck this side of Squaw Creek.
Bet you don't make it before Sunday!"

The outbound conductor's retort was lost
in the clank of couplings as the train
lurched forward on the slippery rails.

"Phebe, is thee awake?" the old gentleman softly called to his daughter, about the
small hours.

"Yes, father. Want anything?"

"Are those ventilators shut? I feel a
cold draft in the back of my berth."

The ventilators were all shut, but the
train was now climbing the Wind River
divide, the cold bitterly increasing, and the
wind dead ahead. Cinders tinkled on the
roaring stovepipes, the blast swept the car
roofs, pelting the window panes with fine,
dry snow, and searching every joint and
crevice defended by the company's uphol-
stery.

Phebe slipped down behind the berth-curtain, and tucked a shawl in at her father's back. Her low voice could be heard, and the old man's self-pitying tones in answer to her tender questionings. He coughed at intervals till daybreak, when there was silence in section No. 7.

In No. 8, across the aisle, the young man lay awake in the strength of his thoughts, and made up passionate sentences which he fancied himself speaking to persons he might never be brought face to face with again. They were people mixed in with his life in various relations, past and present, whose opinions had weighed with him. When he heard Phebe talking to her father, he muttered, with a sort of anguish : —

" Oh, you precious lamb ! "

He and his companion made their toilet early, and breakfasted and smoked together, and their taciturn relation continued as before. Snow filled the air, and blotted out the distance, but there were few stationary dark objects outside by which to gauge its fall. They were across the border now, between Wyoming and Idaho, in a featureless white region, a country of small Mormon ranches, far from any considerable town.

The old man slept behind his curtains.
Phebe went through the morning routine by
which women travelers make themselves at
home and pass the time, but obviously her
day did not begin until her father had reported himself. She had found a hole in
one of her gloves, which she was mending,
choosing critically the needle and the silk
for the purpose from a very complete house-
wife in brown linen bound with a brown
silk galloon. Again the young man was
reminded of his boyhood, and of certain
kind old ladies of precise habits who had
contributed to his happiness, and occasion-
ally had eked out the fond measure of pater-
nal discipline.

The snow continued; about noon the
train halted at a small water station, waited
awhile as if in consideration of difficulties
ahead, and then quietly backed down upon
a side-track. A shock of silence followed.
Every least personal movement in the thinly
peopled car, before lost in the drumming of
the wheels, asserted itself against this new
medium. The passengers looked up and at
one another; the Pullman conductor stepped
out to make inquiries.

The silence continued, and became embarrassing. Phebe dropped her scissors. This time the young man sat still, but the flush rose to his forehead as before. The old gentleman's breathing could be heard behind his curtains; the porter rattling plates in the cooking-closet; the soft rustling of the snow outside. Phebe stepped to her father's berth, and peeped between his curtains; he was still sleeping. Her voice was hushed to the note of a sick-room as she asked, —

" Where are we now, do you know ? "

The young man was looking at her, and to him she addressed the question.

With a glance at his companion, he crossed to her side of the car, and took the seat in front of her.

" We are in the Bear Lake valley, just over the border of Idaho, about fifteen miles from the Squaw Creek divide," he answered, sinking his voice.

" Did you hear what that person said in the night, when a train passed us, about our not getting through ? "

" I wondered if you heard that." He smiled. " You did not rest well, I 'm afraid."

" I was anxious about father. This weather is a great surprise to us. We were told the winters were short in southern Idaho — almost like Virginia ; but look at this ! "

" We have nearly eight thousand feet of altitude here, you must remember. In the valleys it is warmer. There the winter does break usually about this time. Are you going on much farther ? "

" To a place called Volney."

" Volney is pretty high ; but there is Boisé, farther down. Strangers moving into a new country very seldom strike it right the first time."

" Oh, we shall stay at Volney, even if we do not like it ; that is, if we *can* stay. I have a married sister living there. She thought the climate would be better for father."

After a pause she asked, " Do you know why we are stopping here so long ? "

" Probably because we have had orders not to go any farther."

" Do you mean that we are blocked ? "

" The train ahead of us is. We shall stay here until that gets through."

" You seem very cheerful about it," she said, observing his expression.

" Ah, I should think so ! "

His short lip curled in the first smile she had seen upon his strong, brooding face. She could not help smiling in response, but she felt bound to protest against his irresponsible view of the situation.

" Have you so much time to spend upon the road ?   I thought the men of this country were always in a hurry."

" It makes a difference where a man is going, and on what errand, and what fortune he meets with on the way.   *I* am not going to Volney."

She did not understand his emphasis, nor the bearing of his words. His eyes dropped to her hands lying in her lap, still holding the glove she had been mending.

" How nicely you do it ! How can you take such little stitches without pricking yourself, when the train is going ? "

" It is my business to take little stitches. I don't know how to do anything else."

" Do you mean it literally ? It is your business to sew ? "

The notion seemed to surprise him.

"No; I mean in a general sense. Some
of us can do only small things, a stitch at a
time, — take little steps, and not know
always where they are going."

"Is this a little step — to Volney?"

"Oh, no; it is a very long one, and
rather a wild one, I 'm afraid. I suppose
everybody does a wild thing once in a life-
time?"

"How should *you* know that?"

"I only said so. I don't say that it is
true."

"People who take little steps are sometimes picked up and carried off their feet
by those who take long, wild ones."

"Why, what are we talking about?" she
asked herself, in surprise.

"About going to Volney, was it not?"
he suggested.

"What is there about Volney, please tell
me, that you harp upon the name? I am
a stranger, you know; I don't know the
country allusions. Is there anything peculiar about Volney?"

"She is a deep little innocent," he said
within himself; "but oh, so innocent!"
And again he appeared to gather himself

in pained resistance to some thought that
jarred with the thought of Phebe. He rose
and bowed, and so took leave of her, and
settled himself back into his corner, shading
his eyes with his hand.

He ate no luncheon, Phebe noticed, and
he sat so long in a dogged silence that she
began to cast wistful glances across the
aisle, wondering if he were ill, or if she had
unwittingly been rude to him. Any one
could have shaken her confidence in her
own behavior; moreover, she reminded herself, she did not know the etiquette of an
overland train. She had heard that the
Western people were very friendly; no doubt
they expected a frank response in others.
She resolved to be more careful the next
time, if the moody young man should speak
to her again.

Her father was awake now, dressed and
sitting up. He was very chipper, but Phebe
knew that his color was not natural, nor his
breathing right. He was much inclined to
talk, in a rambling, childish, excited manner
that increased her anxiety.

The young man in No. 8 had evidently
taken his fancy; his formal, old-fashioned
advances were modestly but promptly met.

"I suppose it is not usual, in these parts, for travelers to inquire each other's names?" the old gentleman remarked to his new acquaintance; "but we seem to have plenty of time on our hands; we might as well improve it socially. My name is David Underhill, and this is my daughter Phebe. Now what might thy name be, friend?"

"My name is Ludovic," said the youth, looking a half-apology at Phebe, who saw no reason for it.

"First or family name?"

"Ludovic is my family name."

"And a very good name it is," said the old gentleman. "Not a common name in these parts, I should say, but one very well and highly known to me," he added, with pleased emphasis. "Phebe, thee remembers a visit we had from Martin Ludovic when we were living at New Rochelle?"

"Thee knows I was not born when you lived at New Rochelle, father dear."

"True, true! It was thy mother I was thinking of. She had a great esteem for Martin Ludovic. He was one of the world's people, as we say — in the world, but not of the world. Yet he made a great success

in life. He was her father's junior partner
— rose from a clerk's stool in his counting-
room; and a great success he made of it.
But that was after Friend Lawrence's time.
My wife was Phebe Lawrence."

Young Ludovic smiled brightly in reply
to this information, and seemed about to
speak, but the old gentleman forestalled
him.

" Friend Lawrence had made what was
considered a competence in those days — a
very small one it would be called now; but
he was satisfied. Thee may not be aware
that it is a recommendation among the
Friends, and it used to be a common practice,
that when a merchant had made a suffi-
ciency for himself and those depending on
him, he should show his sense of the favor
of Providence by stepping out and leaving
his chance to the younger men. Friend
Lawrence did so — not to his own benefit
ultimately, though that was no one's fault
that ever I heard; and Martin Ludovic was
his successor, and a great and honorable
business was the outcome of his efforts.
Now does thee happen to recall if Martin is
a name in thy branch?"

" My grandfather was Martin Ludovic of the old New York house of Lawrence and Ludovic," said the cadet of that name; but as he gave these credentials a profound melancholy subdued his just and natural pride.

"Is it possible!" Friend Underhill exulted, more pleased than if he had recovered a lost bank-note for many hundreds. There are no people who hold by the ties of blood and family more strongly than the Friends; and Friend Underhill, on this long journey, had felt himself sadly insolvent in those sureties that cannot be packed in a trunk or invested in irrigable lands. It was as if on the wild, cold seas he had crossed the path of a bark from home. He yearned to have speech with this graciously favored young man, whose grandfather had been his Phebe's grandfather's partner and dearest friend. The memory of that connection had been cherished with ungrudging pride through the succeeding generations in which the Ludovics had gone up in the world and the Lawrences had come down. Friend Underhill did not recall — nor would he have thought it of the least importance

— that a Lawrence had been the benefactor in the first place, and had set Martin Ludovic's feet upon the ladder of success. He took the young man's hand affectionately in his own, and studied the favor of his countenance.

"Thee has the family look," he said in a satisfied tone; "and they had no cause, as a rule, to be discontented with their looks."

Young Ludovic's eyes fell, and he blushed like a girl; the dark-red blood dyed his face with the color almost of shame. Phebe moved uneasily in her seat.

"Make room beside thee, Phebe," said her father; "or, no, friend Ludovic; sit thee here beside me. If the train should start, I could hear thee better. And thy name — let me see — thee must be a Charles Ludovic. In thy family there was always a Martin, and then an Aloys, and then a Charles; and it was said — though a foolish superstition, no doubt — that the king's name brought ill luck. The Ludovic whose turn it was to bear the name of the unhappy Stuart took with it the misfortunes of three generations."

"A very unjust superstition I should call it," pronounced Phebe.

"Surely, and a very idle one," her father acquiesced, smiling at her warmth. "I trust, friend Charles, it has been given thee happily to disprove it in thy own person."

"On the contrary," said Charles Ludovic, "if I am not the unluckiest of my name, I hope there may never be another."

He spoke with such conviction, such energy of sadness, only silence could follow the words. Then the old gentleman said, most gently and ruefully : —

"If it be indeed as thee says, I trust it will not seem an intrusion, in one who knew thy family's great worth, to ask the nature of thy trouble — if by chance it might be my privilege to assist thee. I feel of rather less than my usual small importance — cast loose, as it were, between the old and the new ; but if my small remedies should happen to suit with thy complaint, it would not matter that they were trifling — like Phebe's drops and pellets she puts such faith in," he added, with a glance at his daughter's downcast face.

"Dear sir, you *have* helped me, by the

gift of the outstretched hand. Between
strangers, as we are, that implies a faith as
generous as it is rare."

" Nay, we are not strangers; no one of
thy name shall call himself stranger to one
of ours. Shall he, Phebe? Still, I would
not importune thee " —

" I thank you far more than you can
know ; but we need not talk of my troubles.
It was a graceless speech of mine to obtrude
them."

" As thee will. But I deny the lack of
grace. The gracelessness was mine to bring
up a foolish saying, more honored in the
forgetting."

Here Phebe interposed with a spoonful of
the medicine her father had referred to so
disparagingly. " I would not talk any more
now, if I were thee, father. Thee sees how
it makes thee cough."

At this, Ludovic rose to leave them ; but
Phebe detained him, shyly doing the honors
of their quarters in the common caravan.
He stayed, but a constrained silence had
come upon him. The old gentleman closed
his eyes, and sometimes smiled to himself
as he sat so, beside the younger man, and

Phebe had strange thoughts as she looked at them both. Her imagination was greatly stirred. She talked easily and with perfect unconsciousness to Ludovic, and told him little things she could remember having heard about the one generation of his family that had formerly been connected with her own. She knew more about it, it appeared, than he did. And more and more he seemed to lose himself in her eyes, rather than to be listening to her voice. He sat with his back to his companion across the aisle; at length the latter rose, and touched him on the shoulder. He turned instantly, and Phebe, looking up, caught the hard, roused expression that altered him into the likeness of another man.

"I am going outside." No more was said, but Ludovic rose, bowed to Phebe, and followed his curt fellow-passenger.

"What can be the connection between them?" thought the girl. "They seem inseparable, yet not friends precisely. How could they be friends?" And in her prompt mental comparison the elder man inevitably suffered. She began to think of all the tragedies with which young lives are fatalistically bound up; but it was significant that none of her speculations included the possibility of anything in the nature of error in respect to this Charles Ludovic who called himself unhappy.

II

"Stop a moment. I want to speak to you," said Ludovic. The two men were passing through the gentlemen's toilet-room; Ludovic turned his back to the marble wash-stand, and waited, with his head up, and the tips of his long hands resting in his trousers' pockets. "I have a favor to ask of you, Mr. Burke."

"Well, sir, what's the size of it?"

"You must have heard some of our talk in there; you see how it is? They will never, of themselves, suspect the reason of your fondness for my company. Is it worth while, for the time we shall be together, to put them on to it? It's not very easy, you see; make it as easy as you can."

"Have I tried to make it hard, Mr. Ludovic?"

"Not at all. I don't mean that."

"Am I giving you away most of the time?"

"Of course not. You have been most awfully good. But you 're — you 're damnably in my way. I see you out of the corner of my eye always, when you are n't square in front of me. I can't make a move but you jump. Do you think I am such a fool as to make a break now? No, sir; I am going through with this; I 'm in it most of the time. Now see here, I give you my word — and there are no liars of my name — that you will find me with you at Pocatello. Till then let me alone, will you? Keep your eyes off me. Keep out of range of my talk. I would like to say a word now and then without knowing there 's a running comment in the mind of a man across the car, who thinks he knows me better than the people I am talking to — understand?"

"Maybe I do, maybe I don't," said Mr. Burke, deliberately. "I don't know as it 's any of my business what you say to your friends, or what they think of you. All I 'm responsible for is your person."

"Precisely. At Pocatello you will have my person."

"And have I got your word for the road between?"

"My word, and my thanks — if the thanks of a man in my situation are worth anything."

"I 'm dum sorry for you, Mr. Ludovic, and I don't mind doing what little I can to make things easy " — Mr. Burke paused, seeing his companion smile. "Well, yes, I know it 's hard — it 's dooced almighty hard ; and it looks like there was a big mistake somewheres, but it 's no business of mine to say so. Have a cigar ? "

Young Mr. Ludovic had accepted a number of Mr. Burke's palliative offers of cigars during their journey together ; he accepted the courtesy, but he did not smoke the cigars. He usually gave them to the porter. He had an expensive taste in cigars, as in many other things. He paid for his high-priced preferences, or he went without. He was never willing to accept any substitute for the thing he really wanted ; and it was very hard for him, when he had set his heart upon a thing, not to approach it in the attitude that an all-wise Providence had intended it for him.

About dusk the snow-plow engines from above came down for coal and water. They brought no positive word, only that the plows and shovelers were at work at both ends of the big cut, and they hoped the track would be free by daybreak. But the snow was still falling as night set in.

Ludovic and Phebe sat in the shadowed corner behind the curtains of No. 7. Phebe's father had gone to bed early; his cough was worse, and Phebe was treating him for that and for the fever which had developed as an attendant symptom. She was a devotee in her chosen school of medicine; she knew her remedies, within the limits of her household experience, and used them with the courage and constancy that are of no school, but which better the wisdom of them all.

Ludovic observed that she never lost count of the time through all her talk, which was growing more and more absorbing; he was jealous of the interruption when she said, "Excuse me," and looked at her watch, or rose and carried her tumblers of medicine alternately to the patient, and woke him gently; for it was now a case for strenuous treatment, and she purposed to watch out the night, and give the medicines regularly every hour.

Mr. Burke was as good as his word; he kept several seats distant from the young people. He had a private understanding, though, with the car officials: not that he put no faith in the word of a Ludovic, but business is business.

When he went to his berth about eleven o'clock he noticed that his prisoner was still keeping the little Quaker girl company, and neither of them seemed to be sleepy. The table where they had taken supper together was still between them, with Phebe's watch and the medicine tumblers upon it. The panel of looking-glass reflected the young man's profile, touched with gleams of lamplight, as he leaned forward with his arms upon the table.

Phebe sat far back in her corner, pale and grave; but when her eyes were lifted to his face they were as bright as winter stars.

It was Ludovic's intention, before he parted with Phebe, to tell her his story — his own story; the newspaper account of him she would read, with all the world, after she had reached Volney. Meantime he wished to lose himself in a dream of how it might have been could he have met this little Phebe, not on a side-track, his chance already spoiled, but on the main line, with a long ticket, and the road clear before them to the Golden Gate.

Under other circumstances she might not have had the same overmastering fascination for him; he did not argue that question with himself. He talked to her all night long as a man talks to the woman he has chosen and is free to win, with but a single day in which to win her; and underneath his impassioned tones, shading and deepening them with tragic meaning, was the truth he was withholding. There was no one to stand between Phebe and this peril, and how should she know whither they were drifting?

He told her stories of his life of danger and excitement and contrasts, East and West; he told her of his work, his ambitions, his disappointments; he carried her from city to city, from camp to camp. He spoke to sparkling eyes, to fresh, thrilling sympathies, to a warm heart, a large comprehension, and a narrow experience. Every word went home; for with this girl he was strangely sure of himself, as indeed he might have been.

And still the low music of his voice went on; for he did not lack that charm, among many others — a voice for sustained and moving speech. Perhaps he did not know his own power; at all events, he was unsparing of an influence the most deliberate and enthralling to which the girl had ever been subjected.

He was a Ludovic of that family her own had ever held in highest consideration. He was that Charles Ludovic who had called himself unhappiest of his name. Phebe never forgot this fact, and in his pauses, and often in his words, she felt the tug of that strong undertow of unspoken feeling pulling him back into depths where even in thought she could not follow him.

And so they sat face to face, with the watch between them ticking away the fateful moments. For Ludovic, life ended at Pocatello, but not for Phebe.

What had he done with that faith they had given him — the gentle, generous pair! He had resisted, he thought that he was resisting, his mad attraction to this girl —

of all girls the most impossible to him now, yet the one, his soul averred, most obviously designed for him. His wild, sick fancy had clung to her from the moment her face had startled him, as he took his last backward look upon the world he had forfeited.

His prayer was that he might win from Phebe, before he left her at Pocatello, some sure token of her remembrance that he might dwell upon and dream over in the years of his buried life.

It would not have been wonderful, as the hours of that strange night flew by, if Phebe had lost a moment, now and then, had sometimes wandered from the purpose of her vigil. Her thoughts strayed, but they came back duly, and she was constant to her charge. Through all that unwholesome enchantment her hold upon herself was firm, through her faithfulness to the simple duties in which she had been bred.

Meanwhile the train lay still in the darkness, and Ludovic thanked God, shamelessly, for the snow. How the dream outwore the night and strengthened as morning broke gray and cold, and quiet with the stillness of the desert, we need not follow. More

and more it possessed him, and began to
seem the only truth that mattered.

He took to himself all the privileges of
her protector; the rights, indeed — as if he
could have rights such as belong to other '
men, now, in regard to any woman.

If the powers that are named of good or
evil, according to the will of the wisher, had
conspired to help him on, the dream could
not have drawn closer to the dearest facts of
life; but no spells were needed beyond those
which the reckless conjurer himself possessed
—- his youth, his implied misfortunes, his
unlikeness to any person she had known, his
passion, " meek, but wild," which he neither
spoke nor attempted to conceal.

And Phebe sat like a charmed thing while
he wove the dream about her. She could
not think; she had nothing to do while her
father slept; she had nowhere to go, away
from this new friend of her father's choosing. She was exhausted with watching, and
nervously unstrung. Her hands were ice;
her color went and came; her heart was in
a wild alarm. She blushed almost as she
breathed, with his eyes always upon her;
and blushing, could have wept, but for the

pride that still was left her in this strange, unwholesome excitement.

It was an ordeal that should have had no witnesses but the angels; yet it was seen of the porter and the conductor and Mr. Burke. The last was not a person finely cognizant of situations like this one; but he felt it and resented it in every fibre of his honest manhood.

" What's Ludovic doing?" he asked himself in heated soliloquy. " He's out of the running, and the old man's sick abed, and no better than an old woman when he's well. What's the fellow thinking of?"

Mr. Burke took occasion to ask him, when they were alone together — Ludovic putting the finishing touches to a shave; the time was not the happiest, but the words were honest and to the point.

" I did n't understand," said Mr. Burke, " that the little girl was in it. Now, do you call it quite on the square, Mr. Ludovic, between you and her? I don't like it, myself; I don't want to be a party to it. I 've got girls of my own."

Ludovic held his chin up high; his hands shook as he worked at his collar-button.

" Have you got any boys? " he flung out in the tone of a retort.

" Yes ; one about your age, I should guess."

" How would you like to see him in the fix I 'm in ? "

" I could n't suppose it, Mr. Ludovic. My boy and you ain't one bit alike."

" Are your girls like her ? "

" No, sir ; they are not. I ain't worrying about them any, nor would n't if they was in her place. But there 's points about this thing " —

" We 'll leave the points. Suppose, I say, your boy was in my fix : would you grudge him any little kindness he might be able to cheat heaven, we 'll say, out of between here and Pocatello ? "

" Heaven can take care of itself ; that little girl is not in heaven yet. And there 's kindnesses and kindnesses, Mr. Ludovic. There are some that cost like the mischief. I expect you 're willing to bid high on kindness from a nice girl, about now ; but how about her ? Has kindness gone up in her market ? I guess not. That little creetur's goods can wait ; she 'd be on top in any mar-

ket. I guess it ain't quite a square deal between her and you."

Ludovic sat down, and buried his hands
in his pockets. His face was a dark red;
his lips twitched.

"Are you going to stick to your bargain,
or are you not?" he asked, fixing his eyes
on a spot just above Mr. Burke's head.

"You've got the cheek to call it a bargain! But say it was a bargain. I did n't
know, I say, that the little girl was in it.
Your bank's broke, Mr. Ludovic. You
ought to quit business. You've got no right
to keep your doors open, taking in money
like hers, clean gold fresh from the mint."

"O Lord!" murmured Ludovic; and he
may have added a prayer for patience with
this common man who was so pitilessly in
the right. A week ago, and the right had
been easy to him. But now he was off the
track; every turn of the wheels tore something to pieces.

"There are just two subjects I cannot
discuss with you," he said, sinking his voice.
"One is that young lady. Her father knows
my people. She shall know me before I
leave her. They say we shall go through to-

night. You must think I am the devil if you think that, without the right even to dispense with your company, I can have much to answer for between here and Pocatello."

"You are as selfish as the devil, that's what I think; and the worst of it is, you look as white as other folks."

"Then leave me alone, or else put the irons on me. Do one thing or the other. I won't be dogged and watched and hammered with your infernal jaw! You can put a ball through me, you can handcuff me before her face; but my eyes are my own, and my tongue is my own, and I will use them as I please."

Mr. Burke said no more. He had said a good deal; he had covered the ground, he thought. And possibly he had some sympathy, even when he thought of his girls, with the young fellow who had looked too late in the face of joy and gone clean wild over his mischance.

It was his opinion that Ludovic would "get" not less than twenty-five years. There were likely to be Populists on that jury; the prisoner's friends belonged to a clique of big monopolists; it would go harder

with him than if he had been an honest
miner, or a playful cow-boy on one of his
monthly " tears."

When Ludovic returned to his section,
Phebe had gone to sleep in the corner opposite, her muff tucked under one flushed
cheek; the other cheek was pale. Shadows
as delicate as the tinted reflections in the
hollow of a snow-drift slept beneath her chin,
and in the curves around her pathetic eyelids, and in the small incision that defined
her pure red under lip. Again the angels,
whom we used to believe in, were far from
this their child.

Ludovic drew down all the blinds to keep
out the glare, and sat in his own place, and
watched her, and fed his aching dream. He
did not care what he did, nor who saw him,
nor what anybody thought.

In the afternoon he took her out for a
walk. The snow had stopped; her father
was up and dressed, and very much better,
and Phebe was radiant. Her sky was clearing all at once. She charged the porter to
call her in " just twenty minutes," for then
she must give the medicine again. On their
way out of the car Ludovic slipped a dollar

into the porter's hand. Somehow that clever
but corrupted functionary let the time slip
by, to Phebe's innocent amazement. Could
he have gone to sleep? Surely it must be
more than twenty minutes since they had
left the car.

" He 's probably given the dose himself,"
said Ludovic. " A good porter is always
three parts nurse."

" But he does n't know which medicine to
give."

" Oh, let them be," he said impatiently.
" He 's talking to your father, and making
him laugh. He 'll brace him up better
than any medicine. They will call you fast
enough if you are needed."

They walked the platform up and down
in front of the section-house. They were
watched, but Ludovic did not care for that
now.

" Will you take my arm ? "

She hesitated, in amused consideration of
her own inexperience.

" Why, I never *did* take any one's arm
that I remember. I don't think I could keep
step with thee."

The intimate pronoun slipped out un-
awares.

" I will keep step with *thee*."

" I don't know that I quite like to hear you use that word."

. " But you used it, just now, to me."

" It was an accident, then."

" Your father says ' thee ' to me."

" He is of an older generation ; my mother wore the Friends' dress. But those customs had a religious meaning for them to which I cannot pretend. With me it is a sort of instinct ; I can't explain it, nor yet quite ignore it."

" Have I offended that particular instinct of yours which attaches to the word ' thee ' ? "

He seemed deeply chagrined. He was one who did not like to make mistakes, and he had no time to waste in apologizing and recovering lost ground.

" People do say it to us sometimes in fun, not knowing what the word means to us," said Phebe.

In the fresh winter air she was regaining her tone — escaping from him, Ludovic felt, into her own sweet, calm self-possession.

" Then you distinctly refuse me whatever — the least — that word implies ? I am one of those who ' rush in ' ? "

" Oh, no ; but you are much too serious. It is partly a habit of speech ; we cannot lose the habit of speaking to each other as strangers in three days."

" You were never a stranger to me. I knew you from the first moment I saw you ; yet each moment since you have been a fresh surprise."

" I cannot keep up with you," she said, slipping her hand out of his arm. In the grasp of his passionate dream he was striding along regardless, not of her, but of her steps.

" Oh, little steps," he groaned within himself — " oh, little doubting steps, why did we not meet before ? "

Oh, blessed hampering steps, how much safer would his have gone beside them !

" What a charming pair ! " cried a lady passenger from the forward sleeper. She too was walking, with her husband, and her eye had been instantly taken by the gentle girl with the delicate wild-rose color, halting on the arm of a splendid youth with dare-devil eyes, who did not look as happy as he ought with that sweet creature on his arm.

" Is n't it good to know that the old sto-

ries are going on all the same?" said the
sentimental traveler. "What do you say —
will that story end in happiness?"

"I say that he is n't good enough for
her," the husband replied.

"Then he 'll be sure to win her," laughed
the lady. "He has won her, I believe,"
she added more seriously, watching the pair
where they stood together at the far end of
the platform; "but something is wrong."

"Something usually is at that stage, if I
remember. Come, let us get aboard."

The sun was setting clear in the pale
saffron west. The train from the buried
cut had been released, and now came sliding
down the track, welcomed by boisterous sal-
utations. Behind were the mighty snow-
plow engines, backing down, enwreathed
and garlanded with snow.

"A-a-all aboard!" the conductor drawled
in a colloquial tone to the small waiting
group upon the platform.

Slowly they crept back upon the main
track, and heavily the motion increased, till
the old chant of the rails began again, and
they were thundering westward down the
line.

III

Phebe was much occupied with her father, perhaps purposely so, until his bedtime. She made him her innocent refuge. Ludovic kept subtly away, lest the friendly old gentleman should be led into conversation, which might delay the hour of his retiring. He went cheerfully to rest about the time the lamps were lighted, and Phebe sought once more her corner in the empty section, shaded by her father's curtains.

Ludovic, dropping his voice below the roar of the train, asked if he might take the seat beside her.

He took it, and turned his back upon the car. He looked at his watch. He had just three hours before Pocatello. The train was making great speed; they would get in, the conductor said, by eleven o'clock. But he need not tell her yet. Half an hour passed, and his thoughts in the silence were no longer to be borne.

She was aware of his intense excitement, his restlessness, the nervous action of his hands. She shrank from the burning misery in his questioning eyes. Once she heard him whisper under his breath; but the words she heard were, "*My love! my love!*" and she thought she could not have heard aright. Her trouble increased with her sense of some involuntary strangeness in her companion, some recklessness impending which she might not know how to meet. She rose in her place, and said tremulously that she must go.

"Go!" He sprang up. "Go where, in Heaven's name? Stay," he implored, "and be kind to me! We get off at Pocatello."

"We?" she asked with her eyes in his.

"That man and I. I am his prisoner."

She sank down again, and stared at him mutely.

"He is the sheriff of Bingham County, and I am his prisoner," he repeated. "Do the words mean nothing to you?" He paused for some sign that she understood him. She dropped her eyes; her face had become as white as a snowdrop.

"He is taking me to Pocatello for the preliminary examination — oh, must I tell you this? If I thought you would never read it in the ghastly type" —

"Go on," she whispered.

" Examination," he choked, " for — for homicide. I don't know what the judge will call it; but the other man is dead, and I am left to answer for the passion of a moment with my life. And you will not speak to me ? "

But now she did speak. Leaning forward so that she could look him in the eyes, she said : —

" I thought when I saw that man always with you, watching you, that he might be taking you, with your consent, to one of those places where they treat persons for — for unsoundness of the mind. I knew you had some trouble that was beyond help. I could think of nothing worse than that. It haunted me till we began to speak together; then I knew it could not be ; now I wish it had been."

" I do not," said Ludovic. " I thank God I am not mad. There is passion in my blood, and folly, perhaps, but not insanity. No ; I am responsible."

She remained silent, and he continued defensively : —

" But I am not the only one responsible. Can you listen ? Can you hear the particulars? One always feels that one's own case is peculiar; one is never the common sinner, you know.

" I have a friend at Pocatello; he is my partner in business. Two years ago he married a New York girl, and brought her out there to live. If you knew Pocatello, you would know what a privilege it was to have their house to go to. They made me free of it, as people do in the West. There is nothing they could not have asked of me in return for such hospitality; it was an obligation not less sacred on my part than that of family.

" When my friend went away on long journeys, on our common business, it was my place in his absence to care for all that was his. There are many little things a woman needs a man to do for her in a place like Pocatello; it was my pride and privilege to be at all times at the service of this lady. She was needlessly grateful, but she liked me besides: she was one who showed her likes and dislikes frankly. She had grown up in a small, exclusive set of persons who knew one another's grandfathers, and were accustomed to say what they

pleased inside; what outsiders thought did
not matter. She had not learned to be
careful; she despised the need of it. She
thought Pocatello and the people there were
a joke. But there is a serious side even
to Pocatello: you cannot joke with rattle-
snakes and vitriol and slow mines. She
made enemies by her gay little sallies, and
she would never condescend to explain.
When people said things that showed they
had interpreted her words or actions in a
stupid or a vulgar way, she gave the thing
up. It was not her business to adapt herself to such people; it was theirs to understand her. If they could not, then it did
not matter what they thought. That was
her theory of life in Pocatello.

"One night I was in a place — not for
my pleasure — a place where a lady's name
is never spoken by a gentleman. I heard
her name spoken by a fool; he coupled it
with mine, and laughed. I walked out of
the place, and forgot what I was there for
till I found myself down the street with my
heart jumping. That time I did right, you
would say.

"But I met him again. It was at the

depot at Pocatello. I was seeing a man off
— a stranger in the place, but a friend of
my friends; we had dined at their house
together. This other — I think he had
been drinking — I suppose he must have
included me in his stupid spite against the
lady. He made his fool speech again. The
man who was with me heard him, and
looked astounded. I stepped up to him. I
said — I don't know what. I ordered him
to leave that name alone. He repeated it,
and I struck him. He pulled a pistol on
me. I grabbed him, and twisted it out of
his hand. How it happened I cannot tell,
but there in the smoke he lay at my feet.
The train was moving out. My friend
pulled me aboard. The papers said I ran
away. I did not. I waited at Omaha for
Mr. Burke.

"And there I met you, three days ago;
and all I care for now is just to know that
you will not think of me always by that
word."

"What word?"

"Never mind; spare me the word. Look
at me! Do I seem to you at all the same
man?"

Phebe slowly lifted her eyes.

" Is there nothing left of me? Answer me the truth. I have a right to be answered."

" You are the same; but all the rest of it is strange. I do not see how such a thing could be."

" Can you not conceive of one wild act in a man not inevitably always a sinner?"

" Oh, yes; but not that act. I cannot understand the impulse to take a life."

" I did not think of his miserable life; I only meant to stop his talking. He tried to take mine. I wish he had. But no, no; I should have missed this glimpse of you. Just when it is too late I learn what life is worth."

" Do men truly do those things for the sake of women? Were you thinking of your friend's wife when you struck him?"

" I was thinking of the man — what a foul-mouthed fool he was — not fit to" — He stopped, seeing the look on Phebe's face.

" Oh, I 'm impossible, I know, to one like you! It 's rather hard I should have to be compared, in your mind, to a race of men

like your father.   Have you never known
any other men ? "

" I have read of all the men other people
read of.   I have some imagination."

" I suppose you read your Bible."

" Yes: the men in the Bible were not all
of the Spirit; but they worshiped the Spirit
— they were humble when they did wrong."

" Did women ever love them ? "

Phebe was silent.

" Do not talk to me of the Spirit," Ludovic pleaded.   " I am a long way from that.
At least I am not a hypocrite — not yet.
Wait till I am a ' trusty,' scheming for a
pardon.   Can you not give me one word of
simple human comfort?   There are just
forty minutes more."

" What can I say ? "

" Tell me this — and oh, be careful !
Could you, if it were permitted a criminal
like me to expiate his sin in the world
among living men, in human relations with
them — could we ever meet?   Could you
say ' thee ' to me, not as to an afflicted person or a child?   Am I to be only a text,
another instance " —

" Many would not blame you.   Neither

do I blame you, not knowing that life or those people," said Phebe. "But there was One who turned away from the evil-speakers, and wrote upon the sand."

"But those evil-speakers spoke the truth."

"Can a lie be stopped by a pistol-shot? But we need not argue."

"No; I see how it is. I shall be to you only another of the wretched sons of Cain."

"I am thy sister," she said, and gave him her hand.

He held it in his strong, cold, trembling clasp.

"Darling, do you know where I am going? I shall never see you, never again —unless you are like the sainted women of your faith who walked the prisons, and preached to them in bonds."

"Thy bonds are mine: but I am no preacher."

The drowsy lights swayed and twinkled, the wheels rang on the frozen rails as the wild, white wastes flew by.

"Father shall never know it," Phebe murmured. "He shall never know, if I can help it, why you called yourself unhappy."

"Is it such an unspeakable horror to you?" He winced.

"He has not many years to live; it would only be one disappointment more." She was leaning back in her seat; her eyes were closed; she looked dead weary, but patient, as if this too were life, and not more than her share.

"Has your father any money, dear?"

She smiled: "Do we look like people with money?"

"If they would only let me have my hands!" he groaned. "To think of shutting up a great strong fellow like me" —

It was useless to go on. He sat, bitterly forecasting the fortunes of those two lambs who had strayed so far from the green pastures and still waters, when he heard Phebe say softly, as if to herself, —

"We are almost there."

Mr. Burke began to fold his newspapers and get his bags in order. His hands rested upon the implements of his office — he carried them always in his pockets — while he stood balancing himself in the rocking car, and the porter dusted his hat and coat.

The train dashed past the first scattered lights of the town.

" Po-catello ! " the brakeman roared in a voice of triumph, for they were " in " at last.

The porter came, and touched Ludovic on the shoulder.

" Gen'leman says he 's ready, sir."

He rose and bent over Phebe. If she had been like any other girl he must have kissed her, but he dared not. He had prayed for a sign, and he had won it — that look of dumb and lasting anguish in her childlike eyes.

Yet, strange passion of the man's nature, he was not sorry for what he had done.

Mr. Burke took his arm in silence, and steered him out of the car ; both doors were guarded, for he had feared there might be trouble. He was surprised at Ludovic's behavior.

" What 's the matter with him ? " the car-conductor asked, looking after the pair as they walked up the platform together. " Is he sick ? "

" Mashed," said the porter, gloomily ; for Ludovic had forgotten the parting fee. " Regular girl mash, the worst I ever saw."

"He's late about it, if he expects to have any fun," said the conductor; and he began to dance, with his hands in his great-coat pockets, for the night air was raw. He was at the end of his run, and was going home to his own girl, whom he had married the week before.

Friends and family influence mustered strong for Ludovic at the trial six weeks later. His lawyer's speech was the finest effort, it was said, ever listened to by an Idaho jury. The ladies went to hear it, and to look at the handsome prisoner, who seemed to grow visibly old as the days of the trial went by.

But those who are acquainted with the average Western jury need not be told that it was not influence that did it, nor the lawyer's eloquence, nor the court's fine-spun legal definitions, nor even the women's tears. They looked at the boy, and thought of their own boys, or they looked inside, and thought of themselves; and they concluded that society might take its chances with that young man at large. They stayed out an hour, out of respect to their oath, and then brought in a verdict of "Not guilty;" and the audience had to be suppressed.

But after the jury's verdict there is society, and all the tongues that will talk, long after the tears are dry. And then comes God in the silence — and Phebe.

The men all say she is too good for him, whose name has been in everybody's mouth. They say it, even though they do not know the cruel way in which he won her love. But the women say that Phebe, though undeniably a saint (and the "sweetest thing that ever lived"), is yet a woman, incapable of inflicting judgment upon the man she loves.

The case is in her hands now. She may punish, she may avenge, if she will; for Ludovic is the slave of his own remorseless conquest. But Phebe has never discovered that she was wronged. There is something in faith, after all; and there is a good deal in blood, Friend Underhill thinks. "Doubtless the grandson of Martin Ludovic must have had great provocation."

I

WHEN the trumpets at Bisuka barracks sound retreat, the girls in the Meadows cottage, on the edge of the Reservation, begin to hurry with the supper things, and Mrs. Meadows, who has been young herself, says to her eldest daughter, " You go now, Callie ; the girls and I can finish." Which means that Callie's colors go up as the colors on the hill come down ; for soon the tidy infantrymen and the troopers with their yellow stripes will be seen, in the first blush of the afterglow, tramping along the paths that thread the sagebrush common between the barracks and the town ; and Callie's young man will be among them, and he will turn off at the bridge that crosses the acéquia, and make for the cottage gate by a path which he ought to know pretty well by this time.

Callie's young man is Henniker, one of

the trumpeters of K troop, —th cavalry; *the* trumpeter, Callie would say, for though there are two of the infantry and two of the cavalry who stand forth at sunset, in front of the adjutant's office, and blow as one man the brazen call that throbs against the hill, it is only Henniker whom Callie hears. That trumpet blare, most masculine of all musical utterances, goes straight from his big blue-clad chest to the heart of his girl, across the clear-lit evening; but not to hers alone. There is only one Henniker, but there is more than one girl in the cottage on the common.

At this hour, nightly, a small dark head, not so high above the sage as Callie's auburn one, pursues its dreaming way, in the wake of two cows and a half-grown heifer, towards the hills where the town herd pastures. Punctually at the first call it starts out behind the cows from the home corral; by the second it has passed, very slowly, the foot-bridge, and is nearly to the corner post of the Reservation; but when " sound off " is heard, the slow-moving head stops still. The cheek turns. A listening eye is raised; it is black, heavily lashed;

the tip of a silken eyebrow shows against the narrow temple. The cheek is round and young, of a smooth clear brown, richly under-tinted with rose, — a native wild flower of the Northwest. As the trumpets cease, and the gun fires, and the brief echo dies in the hill, the liquid eyes grow sad.

"Sweet, sweet! too sweet to be so short and so strong!" The dumb childish heart swells in the constriction of a new and keener sense of joy, an unspeakable new longing.

What that note of the deep-colored summer twilight means to her she hardly understands. It awakens no thought of expectation for herself, no definite desire. She knows that the trumpeter's sunset call is his good-by to duty on the eve of joy; it is the pæan of his love for Callie. Wonderful to be like Callie; who after all is just like any other girl, — like herself, just as she was a year ago, before she had ever spoken to Henniker.

Henniker was not only a trumpeter, one of four who made music for the small two-company garrison; he was an artist with a personality. The others blew according to tactics, and sometimes made mistakes; Henniker never made mistakes, except that he sometimes blew too well. Nobody with an ear, listening nightly for taps, could mistake when it was Henniker's turn, as orderly trumpeter, to sound the calls. He had the temperament of the joyous art : and with it the vanity, the passion, the forgetfulness, the unconscious cruelty, the love of beauty, and the love of being loved that made him the flirt constitutional as well as the flirt military, — which not all soldiers are, but which all soldiers are accused of being. He flirted not only with his fine gait and figure, and bold roving glances from under his cap-peak with the gold sabres crossed above it; he flirted in a particular and personal as well as promiscuous manner, and was ever new to the dangers he incurred, not to mention those to which his willing victims exposed themselves. For up to this time in all his life Henniker had never yet pursued a girl. There had been no need, and as yet no inducement, for him to take the offensive. The girls all felt his irresponsible gift of pleasing, and forgot to be afraid. Not one of the class of girls he met but

envied Callie Meadows, and showed it by
pretending to wonder what he could see in
her.

It was himself Henniker saw, so no wonder he was satisfied, until he should see himself in a more flattering mirror still. The
very first night he met her, Callie had informed him, with the courage of her bright
eyes, that she thought him magnificent fun ;
and he had laughed in his' heart, and said,
" Go ahead, my dear !" And ahead they
went headlong, and were engaged within a
week.

Mother Meadows did not like it much,
but it was the youthful way, in pastoral
frontier circles like their own ; and Callie
would do as she pleased, — that was Callie's
way. Father Meadows said it was the women's business ; if Callie and her mother
were satisfied, so was he.

But he made inquiries at the post, and
learned that Henniker's record was good in
a military sense. He stood well with his
officers, had no loose, unsoldierly habits, and
never was drunk on duty. He did not save
his pay ; but how much " pay " had Meadows
ever saved when he was a single man ?

And within two years, if he wanted it, the trumpeter was entitled to his discharge. So he prospered in this as in former love affairs that had stopped short of the conclusive step of marriage.

Meta, the little cow-girl, the youngest and fairest, though many shades the darkest, of the Meadows household, was not of the Meadows blood. On her father's side, her ancestry, doubtless, was uncertain ; some said carelessly, " Canada French." Her mother was pure squaw of the Bannock breed. But Mother Meadows, whose warm Scotch-Irish heart nourished a vein of romance together with a feudal love of family, upheld that Meta was no chance slip of the murky half-bloods, neither clean wild nor clean tame. Her father, she claimed to know, had been a man of education and of honor, on the white side of his life, a well-born Scottish gentleman, exiled to the wilderness of the Northwest in the service of the Hudson's Bay Company. And Meta's mother had broken no law of her rudimentary conscience. She had not swerved in her own wild allegiance, nor suffered desertion by her white chief. He had been killed in some obscure frontier fight, and his goods, including the woman and child, were the stake for which he had perished.   But Father Josette, who knew all things and all people of those parts, and had baptized the infant by the sainted name of Margaret, had traced his lost plant of grace and conveyed it out of the forest shades into the sunshine of a Christian white woman's home.   Father Josette — so Mrs. Meadows maintained — had known that the babe would prove worthy of transplantation.

She made room for the little black-headed stranger, with soft eyes like a mouse (by the blessing of God she had never lost a child, and the nest was full,) in the midst of her own fat, fair-haired brood, and cherished her in her place, and gave her a daughter's privilege.

In a wild, woodlandish way Meta was a bit of an heiress in her own right.   She had inherited through her mother a share in the yearly increase of a band of Bannock ponies down on the Salmon meadows; and every season, after grand round-up, the settlement was made, — always with distinct fairness, though it took some time, and a good deal of eating, drinking, and diplomacy, before the business could be accomplished.

" What is a matter of a field worth forty shekels betwixt thee and me?" was the etiquette of the transaction, but the outcome was practically the same as in the days of patriarchal transfers of real estate.

Father Meadows would say that it cost him twice over what the maiden's claim was worth to have her cousins the Bannocks, with their wives and children and horses, camped on his borders every summer; for Meta's dark-skinned brethren never sent her the worth of her share in money, but came themselves with her ponies in the flesh, and spare ponies of their own, for sale in the town; and on Father Meadows was the burden of keeping them all good-natured, of satisfying their primitive ideas of hospitality, and of pasturing Meta's ponies until they could finally be sold for her benefit. No account was kept, in this simple, generous household, of what was done for Meta, but strict account was kept of what was Meta's own.

The Bannock brethren were very proud of their fair kinswoman who dwelt in the tents of Jacob. They called her, amongst themselves, by the name they give to the mariposa lily, the closed bud of which is pure white as the whitest garden lily; but as each Psyche-wing petal opens it is mooned at the base with a dark, purplish stain which marks the flower with startling beauty, yet to some eyes seems to mar it as well. With every new bud the immaculate promise is renewed; but the leopard cannot change his spots nor the wild hill lily her natal stain.

This year the sale of pony flesh amounted to nearly a hundred dollars, which Father Meadows put away for Meta's future benefit, — all but one gold piece, which the mother showed her, telling her that it represented a new dress.

"You need a new white one for your best, and I shall have it made long. You 're filling out so, I don't believe you 'll grow much taller."

Meta smiled sedately. In spite of the yearly object lesson her dark kinsfolk presented, she never classed herself among the hybrids. She accepted homage and tribute from the tribe, but in her consciousness, at this time, she was all white. This was due partly to Mother Meadows's large-hearted

and romantic theories of training, and partly
to an accident of heredity. The woman
who looks the squaw is the squaw, when it
comes to the flowering time of her life. To
Meta had succeeded the temperament of
her mother expressed in the features of her
father; whether Canadian trapper or Scotch
grandee, he had owned an admirable profile.

A great social and musical event took
place that summer in the town, and Meta's
first long dress was finished in time to play
its part, as such trifles will, in the simple
fates of girlhood. It was by far the prettiest dress she had ever put over her head:
the work of a professional, to begin with.
Then its length persuaded one that she was
taller than nature had made her. Its short
waist suited her youthful bust and flat back
and narrow shoulders. The sleeves were
puffed and stood out like wings, and were
gathered on a ribbon which tied in a bow
just above the bend of her elbow. Her
arms were round and soft as satin, and
pinkish-pale inside, like the palms of her
small hands. All her skin, though dark, was
as clear as wine in a colored glass. The
neck was cut down in a circle below her

throat, which she shyly clasped with her hands, not being accustomed to feel it bare. And as naturally as a bird would open its beak for a worm, she exclaimed to Mother Meadows, "Oh, how I wish I had some beads!" And before night she had strung herself a necklace of the gold-colored pompons with silver-gray stems that spangle the dry hills in June, — "butter-balls" the Western children call them, — and, in spite of the laughter and gibes of the other girls, she wore her sylvan ornament on the gala night, and its amazing becomingness was its best defense.

So Meta's first long dress went, in company with three other unenvious white dresses and Father Meadows's best coat, to hear the "Coonville Minstrels," a company of amateur performers representing the best musical talent in the town, who would appear "for one night only," for the benefit of the free circulating library fund.

Henniker was not in attendance on his girl as usual.

"What a pity," the sisters said, "that he should have to be on guard to-night!" But Meta remembered, though she did not say

so, that Henniker had been on guard only
two nights before, so it could not be his turn
again, and that could not explain his absence.

But Callie was as gay as ever, and did
not seem put out, even at her father's ban-
tering insinuations about some other possible
girl who might be scoring in her place.

The sisters were enraptured over every
number on the programme. The performers
had endeavored to conceal their identity under burnt cork and names that were ficti-
tious and humorous, but everybody was com-
paring guesses as to which was which, and
who was who. The house was packed, and
" society " was there. The feminine half of
it did not wear its best frock to the show and
its head uncovered, but what of that! A girl
knows when she is looking her prettiest, and
the young Meadowses were in no way concerned for the propriety of their own appearance. Father Meadows, looking along the
row of smiling faces belonging to him, was as
well satisfied as any man in the house. His
eyes rested longer than usual on little Meta
to-night. He saw for the first time that the
child was a beauty ; not going to be,— she was

one then and there. Her hair, which she was
accustomed to wear in two tightly braided
pigtails down her back, had been released
and brushed out all its stately maiden length,
"crisped like a war steed's encolure." It
fell below her waist, and made her face and
throat look pale against its blackness. A
spot of white electric light touched her chest
where it rose and fell beneath the chain of
golden blossom balls,— orange gold, the cavalry color. She looked like no other girl
in the house, though nearly every girl in
town was there.

Part I. of the programme was finished; a
brief wait,— the curtain rose, and behold
the colored gentlemen from Coonville had
vanished. Only the interlocutor remained,
scratching his white wool wig over a letter
which he begged to read in apology for his
predicament. His minstrelsy had decamped,
and spoilt his show. They wrote to inform
him of the obvious fact, and advised him
facetiously to throw himself upon the indul-
gence of the house, but "by no means to
refund the money."

Poor little Meta believed that she was
listening to the deplorable truth, and won-

dered how Father Meadows and the girls
could laugh.

"Oh, won't there be any second part,
after all?" she despaired; at which Father
Meadows laughed still more, and pinched
her cheek, and some persons in the row of
chairs in front half turned and smiled.

"Goosey," whispered Callie, "don't you
see he's only gassing? This is part of the
fun."

"Oh, is it?" sighed Meta, and she waited
for the secret of the fun to develop.

"Look at your programme," Callie in-
structed her. "See, this is the Impressa-
rio's Predicament. The Wandering Minstrel
comes next. He will be splendid, I can tell
you."

"Mr. Piper Hide-and-Seek," murmured
Meta, studying her programme. "What a
funny name!"

"Oh, you child!" Callie laughed aloud,
but as suddenly hushed, for the sensation of
the evening, to the Meadows party, had
begun.

A very handsome man, in the gala dress of
a stage peasant, of the Bavarian Highlands
possibly, came forward with a short, military

step, and bowed impressively.   There was a
burst of applause from the bluecoats in the
gallery, and much whistling and stamping
from the boys.

"Who is it?" the lady in front whispered to her neighbor.

"One of the soldiers from the post," was
the answer.

"Really!"

But the lady's accent of surprise conveyed nothing, beside the speechless admiration of the Meadows family. Callie, who
had been in the exciting secret all along,
whispered violently with the other girls,
but Meta had become quite cold and shivery.
She could not have uttered a word.

Henniker made a little speech in an assumed accent which astonished his friends
almost more than his theatrical dress and
bearing.   He said he was a stranger, piping
his way through a foreign land, but he could
"spik ze Engleesh a leetle."   Would the
ladies and gentlemen permit him, in the embarrassing absence of better performers, to
present them with a specimen of his poor
skill upon a very simple instrument?   Behold!

He flung back his short cloak, and filled his chest, standing lightly on his feet, with his elbows raised.

No rattling trumpet blast from the artist's lips to-night, but, still and small, sustained and clear, the pure reed note trilled forth. Willow whistles piping in springtime in the stillness of deep meadow lands before the grass is long, or in flickering wood paths before the full leaves darken the boughs — such was the pastoral simplicity of the instrument with which Henniker beguiled his audience. Such was the quality of sound, but the ingenuity, caprice, delicacy, and precision of its management were quite his own. They procured him a wild encore.

Henniker had been nervous at the first time of playing; it would have embarrassed him less to come before a strange house; for there were the captain and the captain's lady, and the lieutenants with their best girls; and forty men he knew were nudging and winking at one another; and there were the bonny Meadowses, with their eyes upon him and their faces all aglow. But who was she, the little big-eyed dark one in their midst? He took her in more coolly as he came before the house the second time; and this time he knew her, but not as he ever had known her before.

Is it one of nature's revenges that in the beauty of their women lurks the venom of the dark races which the white man has put beneath his feet? The bruised serpent has its sting; and we know how, from Moab and Midian down, the daughters of the heathen have been the unhappy instruments of proud Israel's fall; but the shaft of his punishment reaches him through the body of the woman who cleaves to his breast.

That one look of Henniker's at Meta, in her strange yet familiar beauty, sitting captive to his spell, went through his flattered senses like the intoxication of strong drink. He did not take his eyes off her again. His face was pale with the complex excitement of a full house that was all one girl and all hushed through joy of him. She sat so close to Callie, his reckless glances might have been meant for either of them; Callie thought at first they were for her, but she did not think so long.

Something followed on the programme at which everybody laughed, but it meant nothing at all to Meta. She thought the supreme moment had come and gone, when a big Zouave in his barbaric reds and blues marched out and took his stand, back from the footlights, between the wings, and began that amazing performance with a rifle which is known as the "Zouave drill."

The dress was less of a disguise than the minstrel's had been, and it was a sterner, manlier transformation. It brought out the fighting look in Henniker. The footlights were lowered, a smoke arose behind the wings, strange lurid colors were cast upon the figure of the soldier magician.

"The stage is burning!" gasped Meta, clutching Callie's arm.

"It's nothing but red fire. You must n't give yourself away so, Meta; folks will take us for a lot of sagebrushers."

Meta settled back in her place with a fluttering sigh, and poured her soul into this new wonder.

But Henniker was not doing himself justice to-night, his comrades thought. No one present was so critical of him or so proud of him as they. A hundred times he had put himself through this drill before a barrack audience, and it had seemed as if be could not make a break. But to-night his nerve was not good. Once he actually dropped his piece, and a groan escaped the row of uniforms in the gallery. This made him angry; he pulled himself up and did some good work for a moment, and then — "Great Scott! he's lost it again! No, he has n't. Brace up, man!" The rifle swerves, but Henniker's knee flies up to catch it; the sound of the blow on the bone makes the women shiver; but he has his piece, and sends it savagely whirling, and that miss was his last. His head was like the centre of a spinning top or the hub of a flying wheel. He felt ugly from the pain of his knee, but he made a dogged finish, and only those who had seen him at his best would have said that his drill was a failure.

Henniker knew, if no one else did, what had lost him his grip in the rifle act. His eyes, which should have been glued to his work, had been straying for another and yet one more look at Meta. Where she

sat so still was the storm centre of emotion
in the house, and when his eyes approached
her they caught the nerve shock that shook
his whole system and spoiled his fine work.
He cared nothing for the success of his
piping when he thought of the failure of
his drill. The failure had come last, and,
with other things, it left its sting.

On the way home to barracks, the boys
were all talking, in their free way, about
Meta Meadows, — the little broncho, they
called her, in allusion to her great mane of
hair, — which made Henniker very hot.

He would not own that his knee pained
him ; he would not have it referred to, and
was ready, next day, to join the riders in
squad drill, a new feature of which was the
hurdles and ditch-jumping and the mounted
exercises, in which as usual, Henniker had
distinguished himself.

The Reservation is bounded on the south-
east side, next the town, by an irrigation
ditch, which is crossed by as many little
bridges as there are streets that open out
upon the common. (All this part of the
town is laid out in "additions," and is
sparsely built up.) Close to this division

line, at right angles with it, are the dry ditches and hurdle embankments over which the stern young corporals put their squads, under the eye of the captain.

Out in the centre of the plain other squads are engaged in the athletics of horsemanship, — a series of problems in action which embraces every sort of emergency a mounted man may encounter in the rush and throng of battle, and the means of instantly meeting it, and of saving his own life or that of a comrade. So much more is made in these days of the individual powers of the man and horse that it is wonderful to see what an exact yet intelligently obedient combination they have become; no less effective in a charge, as so many pounds of live momentum to be hurled on the bayonet points, but much more self-reliant on scout service, or when scattered singly, in defeat, over a wide, strange field of danger.

On the regular afternoons for squad and troop drill, the ditch bank on the town side would be lined with spectators: ladies in light cotton dresses and beflowered hats, small bare-legged boys and muddy dogs, the small boys' sisters dragging bonnetless babies by the hand, and sometimes a tired mother who has come in a hurry to see where her little truants have strayed to, or a cowboy lounging sideways on his peaked saddle, condescending to look on at the riding of Uncle Sam's boys. The crowd assorts itself as the people do who line the barriers at a bull-fight : those who have parasols, to the shadow; those who have barely a hat, to the sun.

Here, on the field of the gray-green plain, under the glaring tent roof of the desert sky, the national free circus goes on, — to the screaming delight of the small boys, the fear and exultation of the ladies, and the alternate pride and disgust of the officers who have it in charge.

A squad of the boldest riders are jumping, six in line. One can see by the way they come that every man will go over : first the small ditch, hardly a check in the pace; then a rush at the hurdle embankment, the horses' heads very grand and Greek as they rear in a broken line to take it. Their faces are as strong and wild as the faces of the men. Their flanks are slippery with sweat. They clear the hurdles, and stretch out for the wide ditch.

" Keep in line! Don't crowd! " the corporal shouts. They are doing well, he thinks. Over they all go ; and the ladies breathe again, and say to each other how much finer this sport is because it is work, and has a purpose in it.

Now the guidon comes, riding alone, and the whole troop is proud of him. The signal flag flashes erect from the trooper's stirrup ; the horse is new to it, and fears it as if it were something pursuing him ; but in the face of horse and man is the same fixed expression, the sober recklessness that goes straight to the finish. If these do not go over, it will not be for want of the spur in the blood.

Next comes a pale young cavalryman just out of the hospital. He has had a fall at the hurdle week before and strained his back. His captain sees that he is nervous and not yet fit for the work, yet cannot spare him openly. He invents an order, and sends him off to another part of the field where the other squads are manœuvring.

If it is not in the man to go over, it will
not be in his horse, though a poor horse may
put a good rider to shame ; but the measure of
every man and every horse is taken by those
who have watched them day by day.

The ladies are much concerned for the
man who fails, — " so sorry " they are for
him, as his horse blunders over the hurdle,
and slackens when he ought to go free ; and
of course he jibs at the wide ditch, and the
rider saws on his mouth.

" Give him his head ! Where are your
spurs, man ? " the corporal shouts, and adds
something under his breath which cannot be
said in the presence of his captain. In they
go, floundering, on their knees and noses,
horse and man, and the ladies cannot see,
for the dust, which of them is on top ; but
they come to the surface panting, and the
man, whose uniform is of the color of the
ditch, climbs on again, and the corporal's
disgust is heard in his voice as he calls,
" Ne-aaxt ! ' "

It need not be said that no corporal ever
asked Henniker where were *his* spurs. To-
day the fret in his temper fretted his horse,
a young, nervous animal who did not need

to know where his rider's heels were quite so often as Henniker's informed him.

" Is that a non-commissioned officer who is off, and his horse scouring away over the plain?   What a dire mortification," the ladies say, " and what a consolation to the bunglers ! "

No, it is the trumpeter. He was taking the hurdle in a rush of the whole squad ; his check-strap broke, and his horse went wild, and slammed himself into another man's horse, and ground his rider's knee against his comrade's carbine.   It is Henniker who is down in the dust, cursing the carbine, and cursing his knee, and cursing the mischief generally.

The ladies strolled home through the heat, and said how glorious it was and how awfully real, and how one man got badly hurt ; and they described in detail the sight of Henniker limping bareheaded in the sun, holding on to a comrade's shoulder ; how his face was a " ghastly brown white," and his eyes were bloodshot, and his black head dun with dust.

" It was the trumpeter who blew so beautifully the other night, — who hurt his knee in the rifle drill," they said. " It was his knee that was hurt to-day. I wonder if it was the same knee?"

It was the same knee, and this time Henniker went to hospital and stayed there; and being no malingerer, his confinement was bitterly irksome and a hurt to his physical pride.

The post surgeon's house is the last one on the line. Then comes the hospital, but lower down the hill. The officer's walk reaches it by a pair of steps that end in a slope of grass. There are moisture and shade where the hospital stands, and a clump of box-elder trees is a boon to the convalescents there. The road between barracks and canteen passes the angle of the whitewashed fence; a wild syringa bush grows on the hospital side, and thrusts its blossoms over the wall. There is a broken board in the fence which the syringa partly hides.

After three o'clock in the afternoon this is the coolest corner of the hospital grounds; and here, on the grass, Henniker was lying, one day of the second week of his confinement.

He had been half asleep when a soft, light thump on the grass aroused him. A stray kitten had crawled through the hole in the fence, and, feeling her way down with her forepaws, had leaped to the ground beside him.

" Hey, pussy ! " Henniker welcomed her pleasantly, and then was silent. A hand had followed the kitten through the hole in the fence, — a smooth brown hand no bigger than a child's, but perfect in shape as a woman's. The small fingers moved and curled enticingly.

" Pussy, pussy ? Come, pussy ! " a soft voice cooed. " Puss, puss, puss ? Come, pussy ! " The fingers groped about in empty air. " Where are you, pussy ? "

Henniker had quietly possessed himself of the kitten, which, moved by these siren tones, began to squirm a little and meekly to " miew." He reached forth his hand and took the small questing one prisoner ; then he let the kitten go. There was a brief speechless struggle, quite a useless one.

" Let me go ! Who is it ? Oh *dear !* "

Another pull. Plainly, from the tone, this last was feminine profanity.

Silence again, the hand struggling persistently, but in vain. The soft bare arm, working against the fence, became an angry red.

" Softly now. It's only me. Did n't you know I was in hospital, Meta ? "

" Is it you, Henniker ? "

" Indeed it is. You would n't begrudge me a small shake of your hand, after all these days ? "

" But you are not in hospital now ? "

" That 's what I am. I 'm not in bed, but I 'm going on three legs when I 'm going at all. I 'm a house-bound man." A heavy sigh from Henniker.

" Have n't you shaken hands enough now, Henniker ? " beseechingly from the other side. " I only wanted kitty ; please put her through the fence."

" What 's your hurry ? "

" Have you got her there ? Callie left her with me. I must n't lose her. Please ? "

" Has Callie gone away ? "

" Why, yes, did n't you know ? She has gone to stay with Tim's wife." (Tim Meadows was the eldest, the married son of the family.) " She has a little baby, and

they can't get any help, and father would n't
let mother go down because it's bad for her
to be over a cook stove, you know."

"Yes, I know the old lady feels the
heat."

"We are quite busy at the house. I
came of an errand to the quartermaster-
sergeant's, and kitty followed me, and the
children chased her. I must go home now,"
urged Meta. "Really, I did not think you
would be so foolish, Henniker. I can't see
what fun there is in this!"

"Yes, but Meta, I've made a discovery,
— here in your hand."

"In my hand? What is it? Let me
see." A violent determined pull, and a
sound like a smothered explosion of laughter
from Henniker.

"Softly, softly now. You'll hurt yourself, my dear."

"Is my hand dirty? It was the kitten,
then; her paws were all over sand."

"Oh, no. Great sign! It's worse than
that. It'll not come off."

"I *will* see what it is!"

"But you can't see unless I was to tell
you. I'm a hand reader, did you know it?

I can tell your fortune by the lines on your palm. I'm reading them off here just like a book."

" Good gracious! what do you see ? "

" Why, it's a most extraordinary thing! Your head line is that mixed up with your heart line, 'pon me word I can't tell which is which. Which is it, Meta? Do you choose your friends with your head entirely, or is it the other way with you, dear? "

" Oh, is that all? I thought you could tell fortunes really. I don't care what I *am ;* I want to know what I'm going to *do.* Don't you see anything that's going to happen to me ? "

" Lots of things. I see something that's going to happen to you right now. I wonder did it ever happen to you before? "

" What is it? When is it coming? "

" It has come. I will put it right here in your hand. But I shall want it back again, remember; and don't be giving it away, now, to anybody else."

A mysterious pause. Meta felt a breath upon her wrist, and a kiss from a mustached lip was pressed into the hollow of her hand.

" Keep that till I ask you for it," said

Henniker quite sternly, and closed her hand tight with his own. The hand became an expressive little fist.

"I think you are just as mean and silly as you can be! I 'll never believe a word you say again."

"Pussy," remarked Henniker, in a mournful aside, "go ask your mistress will she please forgive me. Tell her I 'm not exactly sorry, but I could n't help it. Faith, I could n't."

"I 'm not her mistress," said Meta.

It was a keen reminder, but Henniker did not seem to feel it much.

"Go tell Meta," he corrected. "Ask her please to forgive me, and I 'll take it back, — the kiss, I mean."

"I 'm going now," said Meta. "Keep the kitten, if you want her. She is n't mine, anyway."

But now the kitten was softly crowded through the fence by Henniker, and Meta, relenting, gathered her into her arms and carried her home.

It was certainly not his absence from Callie's side that put Henniker in such a bad humor with his confinement. He grew

morbid, and fell into treacherous dreaming,
and wondered jealously about the other boys,
and what they were doing with themselves
these summer evenings, while he was loafing
on crutches under the hospital trees. He
was frankly pining for his freedom before
Callie should return. He wanted a few
evenings which he need not account for to
anybody but himself; and he got his freedom, unhappily, in time to do the mischief
of his dream, — to put vain, selfish longings
into the simple heart of Meta, and to spoil
his own conscience toward his promised wife.

Henniker knew the ways of the Meadows
cottage as well as if he had been one of the
family. He knew that Meta, having less
skill about the house than the older girls,
took the part of chore-boy, and fetched and
drove away the cows.

It were simple enough to cross her evening track through the pale sagebrush, which
betrayed every bit of contrasting color, the
colors of Meta's hair-ribbon and her evening
frock; it were simple enough, had she been
willing to meet him. But Meta had lost
confidence in the hero of the household.
She had seen Henniker in a new light; and

whatever her heart line said, her head line
told her that she had best keep a good
breadth of sagebrush between herself and
that particular pair of broad blue shoulders
that moved so fast above it. So as Henniker advanced the girl retreated, obscurely,
with shy doublings and turnings, carefully
managed not to reveal that she was running away; for that might vex Henniker,
and she was still too loyal to the family
bond to wish to show her sister's lover an
open discourtesy. She did not dream of the
possibility of his becoming her own lover,
but she thought him capable of going great
lengths in his very peculiar method of teasing.

As soon as he understood her tactics
Henniker changed his own. Without another glance in her direction he made off for
the hills, but not too far from the trail the
cows were taking; and choosing a secluded
spot, behind a thickset clump of sage, he
took out his rustic pipe and waited, and
when he saw her he began to play.

Meta's heart jumped at the first note.
She stole along, drinking in the sounds, no
one molesting or making her afraid. Ahead
of her, as she climbed, the first range of

hills cast a glowing reflection in her face; but the hills beyond were darker, cooler, and the blue-black pines stood out against the sky-like trees of a far cloud-country cut off by some aerial gulf from the most venturesome of living feet.

Henniker saw the girl coming, her face alight in the primrose glow, and he threw away all moments but the present. His breath stopped; then he took a deep inspiration, laid his lips to the pipe, and played, softly, subtly, as one who thinks himself alone.

She had discovered him, but she could not drag herself very far away from those sounds. At last she sat down upon the ground, and gave herself up to listening. A springy sagebush supported her as she let herself sink back; one arm was behind her head, to protect it from the prickly shoots.

" Meta," said Henniker, " are you listening? I 'm talking to you now."

It was all the same: his voice was like another phrase of music. He went on playing, and Meta did not stir.

Another pause. " Are you there still, Meta? I was lonesome to-night, but you ran away from me. Was that friendly? You like my music; then why don't you like me? Well, here's for you again, ungrateful!" He went on playing.

The cows were wandering wide of the trail, towards the upper valley. Meta began to feel herself constrained, and not in the direction of her duty. She rose, cast her long braids over her shoulder, and moved resolutely away.

Henniker was absorbed in what he was saying to her with his pipe. When he had made a most seductive finish he paused, and spoke. He rose and looked about him. Meta was a long way off, down the valley, walking fast. He bounded after her, and caught her rudely around the waist.

" See here, little girl, I won't be made game of like this! I was playing to you, and you ran off and left me tooting like a fool. Was that right?"

" I had to go; it is getting late. The music was too sweet. It made me feel like I could cry." She lifted her long-lashed eyes swimming in liquid brightness. Henniker caught her hand in his.

" I was playing to you, Meta, as I play

to no one else. Does a person steal away and leave another person discoursin' to the empty air ? I did n't think you would want to make a fool of me."

Meta drew away her hand and pressed it in silence on her heart. No woman of Anglo-Saxon blood, without a vast amount of training, could have said so much and said it so naturally with a gesture so hackneyed.

Henniker looked at her from under his eyebrows, biting his mustache. He took a few steps away from her, and then came back.

"Meta," he said, in a different voice, "what was that thing you wore around your neck, the other night, at the minstrels, — that filigree gold thing, eh ? "

The girl looked up, astonished; then her eyes fell, and she colored angrily. No Indian or dog could hate to be laughed at more than Meta; and she had been so teased about her innocent make - believe necklace ! Had the girls been spreading the joke ? She had suddenly outgrown the childish good faith that had made it possible for her to deck herself in it, and she wished never to hear the thing mentioned again. She hung her head and would not speak.

Henniker's suspicions were characteristic. Of course a girl like that must have a lover. Her face confessed that he had touched upon a tender spot.

" It was a pretty thing," he said coldly. " I wonder if I could get one like it for Callie ? "

" I don't think Callie would wear one even if you gave it to her," Meta answered with spirit.

" I say, won't you tell me which of the boys it is, Meta ? — Won't I wear the life out of him, just ! " he added to himself.

" Is what ? "

" Your best fellah ; the one who gave you that."

" There is n't any. It was nothing. I won't tell you what it was ! I made it myself, there ! It was only ' butterballs.' "

" Oh, good Lord ! " laughed Henniker.

Meta thought he was laughing at her. It was too much ! The sweetness of his music was all jangled in her nerves. Tears would come, and then more tears because of the first.

Had Meta been the child of her father,
she might have been sitting that night in
one of the vine-shaded porches of the houses
on the line, with a brace of young lieutenants
at her feet, and in her wildest follies with
them she would have been protected by all
the traditions and safeguards of her class.
As she was the child of her mother, instead, she was out on the hills with Henniker. And how should the squaw's daughter
know the difference between protection and
pursuit ?

When Henniker put his arm around her
and kissed the tears from her eyes, she would
not have changed places with the proudest
lady of the line, — captain's wife, lieuten-
ant's sweetheart, or colonel's daughter of
them all. Her chief, who blew the trumpet,
was as great a man in Meta's eyes as the
officer who buckled on his sabre in obedience
to the call.

As for Henniker, no girl's head against
his breast had ever looked so womanly dear
as Meta's ; no shut eyelids that he had ever
kissed had covered such wild, sweet eyes.
He did not think of her at all in words, any
more than of the twilight afterglow in which

they parted, with its peculiar intensity, its
pang of color.   He simply felt her ; and it
was nearest to the poetic passion of any
emotion that he had ever known.

That night Meta deceived her foster-
mother, and lying awake beside Callie's
empty cot, in the room which the two girls
shared together, she treacherously prayed
that it might be long before her sister's
return.   The wild white lily had opened,
and behold the stain !

It had been a hard summer for Tim
Meadows's family, — the second summer on
a sagebrush ranch, their small capital all in
the ground, the first hay crop ungathered,
and the men to board as well as to pay.
The boarding was Mrs. Tim's part ; yet
many a young wife would have thought that
she had enough to do with her own family
to cook and wash for, and her first baby
to take care of.

" You 'll get along all right," the older
mothers encouraged her.   " A summer baby
is no trouble at all."

No trouble when the trouble is twenty
years behind us, among the joys of the past.
But Tim's wife was wondering if she could

hold out till cool weather came, when the rush of the farm work would be over, and her "summer baby" would be in short clothes and able to sit alone. The heat in their four-roomed cabin, in the midst of the treeless land, was an ordeal alone. To sleep in the house was impossible ; the rooms and the windows were too small to admit enough air. They moved their beds outside, and slept like tramps under the stars ; and the broad light awoke them at earliest dawn, and the baby would never sleep till after ten at night, when the dry Plains wind began to fan the face of the weary land. Even Callie, whose part in the work was subsidiary, lost flesh, and the roses in her cheeks turned sallow, in the month she stayed on the ranch ; but she would have been ashamed to complain, though she was heartsick for a word from Henniker. He had written to her only once.

It was Mrs. Meadows who thought it high time that Callie should come home. She had found a good woman to take her daughter's place, and arranged the matter of pay herself. Tim had said they could get no help, but his mother knew what that meant; such help as they could afford to pay for was worse than none.

It seemed a poor return to Callie, for her sisterly service in the valley, to come home and find her lover a changed man. Mrs. Meadows said he was like all the soldiers she had ever known, — light come, light go. But this did not comfort Callie much, nor more to be reminded what a good thing it was she had found him out in time.

Henniker was not scoundrel enough to make love to two girls at once, two semi-sisters, who slept in the same room and watched each other's movements in the same looking-glass. It was no use pretending that he and Callie could " heat their broth over again; " so the coolness came speedily to a breach, and Henniker no longer openly, in fair daylight, took the path to the cottage gate. But there were other paths.

He had found a way to talk to Meta with his trumpet. He sent her messages at guard-mounting, as the guard was forming, when, as senior trumpeter, he was allowed a choice in the airs he played; and when he was orderly trumpeter, and could not come

himself to say it, he sent her his good-night
in the plaintive notes of taps.

This was the climax of Henniker's flirta-
tions : all that went before had been as
nothing, all that came after was not much
worse than nothing. It was the one sincere
as it was the one poetic passion of his life ;
and had it not cost him his self-respect
through his baseness to Callie, and the
treachery and dissimulation he was teaching
to an innocent child, it might have made
him a faithful man. As it was, his soldier's
honor slept ; it was the undisciplined part
of him that spoke to the elemental nature of
the girl ; and it was fit that a trumpet's
reckless summons, or its brief inarticulate
call, like the note of a wild bird to its mate,
should be the language of his love.

Retreat had sounded, one evening in
October, but it made no stir any more in
the cottage where the girls had been so gay.
Callie, putting the tea on the table, remembered, as she heard the gun fire, how in the
the spring Henniker had said that when
" sound off " was at six he would drop in to
supper some night, and show her how to

make *chili con carne*, a dish that every soldier knows who has served on the Mexican border. Her face grew hard, for these foolish, unsleeping reminders were as constant as the bugle calls.

The women waited for the head of the house; but as he did not come, they sat down and ate quickly, saving the best dish hot for him.

They had finished, and the room was growing dusk, when he came in breezily, and called at once, as a man will, for a light. Meta rose to fetch it. The door stood open between the fore-room and the kitchen, where she was groping for a lamp. Mr. Meadows spoke in a voice too big for the room. He had just been conversing across the common with the quartermaster-sergeant, as the two men's footsteps diverged by separate paths to their homes.

" I hear there's going to be a change at the post; " he shouted. " The —th is going to leave this department, and C troop of the Second is coming from Custer. Sergeant says they are looking for orders any day now."

Mrs. Meadows, before she thought,

glanced at Callie. The girl winced, for she hated to be looked at like that. She held up her head and began to sing audaciously, drumming with her fingers on the table : —

> " ' When my mother comes to know
> That I love the soldiers so,
> She will lock me up all day,
> Till the soldiers march away.' "

"What sort of a song is that?" asked her father sharply.

Callie looked him in the eyes. "Don't you know that tune?" said she. "Henniker plays that at guard-mount; and sometimes he plays this : —

> ' Oh, whistle, and I 'll come to you, my lad,
> Though father and mither and a' should go mad.' "

"Let him play what he likes," said the father angrily. "His saucy jig tunes are nothing to us. I 'm thankful no girl of mine is following after the army. It 's a hard life for a woman, I can tell you, in the ranks."

Callie pushed her chair back, and looked out of the window as if she had not heard.

"Where 's Meta with that lamp? Go and see what 's keeping her."

"Sit still," said Mrs. Meadows. Sho

went herself into the kitchen, but no one heard her speak a word; yet the kitchen was not empty.

There was a calico-covered lounge that stood across the end of the room ; Meta sat there, quite still, her back against the wall. Mrs. Meadows took one look at her; then she lighted the lamp and carried it into the dining-room, and went back and shut herself in with Meta.

"'When my mother comes to know,'

hummed Callie.   Her face was pale.   She hardly knew that she was singing.

"Stop that song!" her father shouted. "Go and see what's the matter with your sister."

"Sister?" repeated Callie.   "Meta is no sister of mine."

"She's your tent-mate, then.   Ye grew nest-ripe under the same mother's wing."

"Meta can use her own wings now, you will find.   She grew nest-ripe very young."

Father Meadows knew that there was trouble inside of that closed door, as there was trouble inside the white lips and shut heart of his frank and joyous Callie, but it

was "the women's business." He went
out to attend to his own.

Irrigation on the scale of a small cottage
garden is tedious work. It has intervals of
silence and leaning on a hoe while one little
channel fills or trickles into the next one;
and the water must be stopped out here, and
floated longer there, like the bath over the
surface of an etcher's plate. Water was
scarce and the rates were high that summer,
and there was a good deal of "dry-point"
work with a hoe in Father Meadows's garden.

He had come to one of the discouraging
places where the ground was higher than the
water could be made to reach without a deal
of propping and damming with shovelfuls of
earth. This spot was close to the window
of the kitchen chamber, which was "mother's
room." She was in there talking to Meta.
Her voice was deep with the maternal note
of remonstrance; Meta's was sharp and high
with excitement and resistance. Her faint-
ness had passed, but Mother Meadows had
been inquiring into causes.

"I am married to him, mother! He is
my husband as much as he can be."

"It was never Father Magrath married

you, or I should be knowing to it before now."

"No; we went before a judge, or a justice, in the town."

"In town! Well, that is something; but be sure there is a wrong or a folly somewhere when a man takes a young girl out of her home and out of her church to be married. If Henniker had taken you 'soberly, in the fear of God'" —

"He *was* sober!" cried Meta. "I never saw him any other way."

"Mercy on us! I was not thinking of the man's habits. He's too good to have done the way he has. That's what I have against him. I don't know what I shall say to Father Josette. The disgrace of this is on me, too, for not looking after my house better. 'Never let her be humbled through her not being all white,' the father said when he brought you to me, and God knows I never forgot that your little heart was white. I trusted you as I would one of my own, and was easier on you for fear of a mother's natural bias toward her own flesh and blood; and now to think that you would lie to me, and take a man in secret that had deceived your sister before you, — as if nothing mattered so that you got what you wanted! And down in the town, without the priest's blessing or a kiss from any of us belonging to you! It's one way to get married, but it's not the right way."

"Did no white girl ever do as I have?" asked Meta, with a touch of sullenness.

"Plenty of them, but they didn't make their mothers happy."

Meta stirred restively on the bed. "Will Father Magrath have to talk to me, and Father Josette, and *all* the fathers?" she inquired. "He said he never would have married Callie anyway, — not even if he couldn't have had me."

"And the more shame to him to say such a thing to one sister of another! Callie is much the best off of you two." Mrs. Meadows rose and moved heavily away from the bed. "Well," she said, "most marriages are just one couple more. It's very little of a sacrament there is about the common run of such things, but I hoped for something better when it came to my girls' turn. However, sorrow is the sacrament God sends us, to give us a chance to

learn a little something before we die. I
expect you 'll learn your lesson."

She came back to the bed, and Meta
moaned as she sat down again, to signify
that she had been talked to enough. But
the mother had something practical to say,
though she could not say it without emo-
tional emphasis, for her outraged feelings
were like a flood that has come down, but
has not yet subsided.

" If there 's any way for you to go with
Henniker when the troop goes, it 's with him
you ought to be; but if he has married
without his captain's consent, he 'll get no
help at barracks. Do you know how that
is, Meta ? "

Meta shook her head; but presently she
forced herself to speak the truth. She did
know that Henniker had told no one at the
post of his marriage. She had never asked
him why, nor had thought that it mattered.

" Oh my ! I was afraid of that," said
Mrs. Meadows. " The colonel knows it was
Callie he was engaged to. Father went up
to see him about Henniker, and the colonel
as good as gave his word for him that he
was a man we could have in the family. A

commanding officer does n't like such go-
ings-on with respectable neighbors."

Mrs. Meadows possibly overestimated the
post commandant's interest in these matters,
but she had gratefully remembered his civil-
ity to her husband when he went to make
fatherly inquiries. The colonel was a father himself, and had seemed to appreciate
their anxiety about Callie's choice. It was
just as well that Meta should know that
none of the constituted authorities were on
the side of her lover's defection.

Meta said nothing to all this. It did not
touch her, only as it bore on the one question, Was Henniker going to leave her behind him?

"How long is it since you have seen him,
that he has n't told you this news himself?"
asked the mother.

"Last night; but perhaps he did not
know."

Henniker had known, as Mrs. Meadows
supposed, but having to shift for himself
in the matter of transportation for the wife
he had never acknowledged, and seeing no
way of providing for her without considerable inconvenience to himself, he had put

off the pain of breaking to her the parting that must come. In their later consultations Meta had mentioned her " pony money," as she called it, and Henniker had privately welcomed the existence of such a fund. It lightened the pressure of his own responsibility in the future, in case — but he did not formulate his doubts. There are more uncertainties than anything else, except hard work, in the life of an enlisted man.

Father Meadows purposely would not speak of Meta's resources. He felt that Henniker had not earned his confidence in this or any other respect where his girls were concerned. Till Meta should come of age, — she was barely sixteen, — or until it could be known what sort of a husband she had got in Henniker, her bit of money was safest in her guardian's hands.

So the orders came, and the transfer of troops was made ; and now it was the trumpeter of C troop that sounded the calls, and Henniker's bold messages at guard-mounting and his tender good-night at taps called no more across the plain. The summer lilies were all dead on the hills, and the common was white with snow. But something in Meta's heart said, —

" ' Weep no more !   Oh, weep no more !
Young buds sleep in the root's white core.' "

And she dried her eyes.   The mother was
very gentle with her; and Callie, hard-eyed,
saying nothing, watched her, and did her
little cruel kindnesses that cut to the quick
of her soreness and her pride.

When the Bannock brethren came, late
in September, the next year, she walked the
sagebrush paths to their encampment with
her young son in her arms.   They looked
at the boy and said that it was good; but
when they asked after the father, and Meta
told them that he had gone with his troop
to Fort Custer, and that she waited for word
to join him, they said it was not good, and
they turned away their eyes in silence from
her shame.   The men did, but the women
looked at her in a silence that said different
things.   Her heart went out to them, and
their dumb soft glances brought healing
to her wounds.   What sorrow, what humili-
ation, was hers that they from all time had
not known?   The men took little notice of
her after that: she had lost caste both as
maid and wife; she was nothing now but
a means of existence to her son.   But be-

tween her and her dark sisters the natural bond grew strong. Old lessons that had lain dormant in her blood revived with the force of her keener intelligence, and supplanted later teachings that were of no use now except to make her suffer more.

It was impossible that Mother Meadows should not resent the wrong and insult to her own child; she felt it increasingly as she came to realize the girl's unhappiness. It grew upon her, and she could not feel the same towards Meta, who kept herself more and more proudly and silently aloof. She was one alone in the house, where no one spoke of the past to reproach her, where nothing but kindness was ever shown. The kindness was like the hand of pardon held out to her. Why did they think she wanted their forgiveness? She was not sorry for what she had done. She wanted nothing, only Henniker. So she crept away with her child and sat among the Bannock women, and was at peace with them whom she had never injured; who beheld her unhappiness, but did not call it her shame.

When she walked the paths across the common, her eyes were always on the sky-

ward range of hills that appeared to her
farther away than ever,—beyond a wider
gulf, now that their tops were white, and
the clouds came low enough to hide them.
Often yellow gleams shot out beneath the
clouds and turned the valleys green. It
seemed to her that Henniker was there; he
was in the cold, bright north, and the trumpets called her, but she could not go, for the
way was very long. Such words as these
she would sometimes whisper to her dark
sisters by the camp-fire, and once they said
to her, "Get strong and go; we will show
you the way."

Henniker was taking life as it comes to
an enlisted man in barracks. He thought
of Meta many times, and of his boy, very
tenderly and shamefully; and if he could
have whistled them to him, or if a wind
of luck could have blown them thither, he
would have embraced them with joy, and
shared with them all that he had. There
was the difficulty. He had so little besides
the very well fitting clothes on his back.
His pay seemed to melt away, month by
month, and where it went to the mischief

only knew. Canteen got a good deal of it. Henniker was one of the popular men in barracks, with his physical expertness, his piping and singing and story-telling, and his high good humor at all times with himself and everybody else. He did not drink much, except in the way of comradeship, but he did a good deal of that. He was a model trumpeter, and a very ornamental fellow when he rode behind his captain on full-dress inspection, more bedight than the captain himself with gold cords and tags and bullion; but he was not a domestic man, and the only person in the world who might perhaps have made him one was a very helpless, ignorant little person, and — she was not there.

It was a bad season for selling ponies. The Indians had arrived late with a larger band than usual, which partly represented an unwise investment they had made on the strength of their good fortune the year before. Certain big ditch enterprises had been starting then, creating a brisk demand for horses at prices unusual, especially in the latter end of summer. This year the big ditch had closed down, and was selling

its own horses, or turning them out upon
the range, and unbroken Indian ponies
could hardly be given away.

The disappointment of the Bannocks was
very great, and their comprehension of
causes very slow. It took some time for
them to satisfy themselves that Father
Meadows was telling them a straight tale.
It took still more time for consultations
as to what should now be done with their
unsalable stock. The middle of October
was near, and the grumbling chiefs finally
decided to accept their loss and go hunting.
The squaws and children were ordered
home to the Reservation by rail, as wards
of the nation travel, to get permission of
the agent for the hunt, and the men, with
ponies, were to ride overland and meet the
women at Eagle Rock.

Thus Meta learned how an Indian woman
may pass unchallenged from one part of the
country to another, clothed in the freedom
of her poverty. In this way the nation
acknowledges a part of its ancient indebt-
edness to her people. No word had come
from Henniker, though he had said that he
should get his discharge in October. Meta's

resolve was taken. The Bannock women encouraged her, and she saw how simple it would be to copy their dress and slip away with them as far as their roads lay together; and thence, having gained practice in her part and become accustomed to its disguises, to go on alone to Custer, where her chief, her beautiful trumpeter, was sounding his last calls. She was wise in this resolution — to see her husband, at whatever cost, before the time of his freedom should come; but she was late in carrying it out.

Long before, she had turned over fruitlessly in her mind every means of getting money for this journey besides the obvious way of asking Father Meadows for her own. She had guessed that her friends were suspicious of Henniker's good faith, and believed that if they should come to know of her intention of running away to follow him they would prevent her for her own good, — which was quite the case.

That was the point Father Meadows made with his wife, when she argued that Meta, being a married woman now, ought to learn the purchasing power of money and its limitations by experimenting with a little of her own.

"We shall do wrong if we keep her a child now," she said.

"But if she has money, she'll lay it by till she gets enough to slip off to her soldier with. There's that much Injun about her; she'll follow to heel like a dog."

Father Meadows could not have spoken in this way of Meta a year ago. She had lost caste with him, also.

"Don't, father," the mother said, with a hurt look. "She'll not follow far with ten dollars in her pocket; but that much I want to try her with. She's like a child about shopping. She'll take anything at all, if it looks right and the man persuades her. And those Jew clerks will charge whatever they think they can get."

Mrs. Meadows had her way, and the trial sum was given to Meta one day, and the next day she and the child were missing.

At dusk, that evening, a group of Bannock squaws, more or less encumbered with packs, and children, climbed upon one of the flat cars of a freight train bound for Pocatello. The engine steamed out of the station, and down the valley, and away upon the autumn plains. The next morning the

Bannocks broke camp, and vanished before the hoar frost had melted from the sage. Their leave-taking had been sullen, and their answers to questions about Meta, with which Father Meadows had routed them out in the night, had been so unsatisfactory that he took the first train to the Fort Hall Agency. There he waited for the party of squaws from Bisuka; but when they came, Meta was not with them. They knew nothing of her, they said; even the agent was deceived by their counterfeit ignorance. They could tell nothing, and were allowed to join their men at Eagle Rock, to go hunting into the wild country around Jackson's Hole.

Father Meadows went back and relieved his wife's worst fear, — that the girl had fulfilled the wrong half of her destiny, and gone back to hide her grief in the bosom of her tribe.

" Then you 'll find her at Custer," said she. " You must write to the quarter-master - sergeant. And be sure you tell him she 's married to him. He may be carrying on with some one else by this time."

Traveling as a ward of the nation travels;
suffering as a white girl would suffer, from
exposure and squalor, weariness and dirt,
but bearing her misery like a squaw, Meta
came at last to Custer station. In five
days, always on the outside of comforts that
other travelers pay for, she had passed from
the lingering mildness of autumn in southern
Idaho into the early winter of the hard
Montana north.

She was fit only for a sick-bed when she
came into the empty station at Custer,
and learned that she was still thirty miles
away from the fort. In her make-believe
broken English, she asked a humble question
about transportation. The station-keeper
was called away that moment by a summons from the wire. It was while she stood
listening to the tapping of the message, and
waiting to repeat her question, that she felt
a frightening pain, sharp, like a knife stick-
ing in her breast. She could take only
short breaths, yet longed for deep ones to
brace her lungs and strengthen her sick
heart. She stepped outside and spoke to a
man who was wheeling freight down the
platform. She dared not throw off her

fated disguise and say, "I am the wife of Trumpeter Henniker. How shall I get to the fort?" for she had stolen a ride of a thousand miles, and she knew not what the penalty of discovery might be. She had borrowed a squaw's wretched immunity, and she must pay the price for that which she had rashly coveted. She pulled her blanket about her face and muttered, "Which way — Fort Custer?"

The freight man answered by pointing to the road. Dark wind clouds rolled along the snow-white tops of the mountains. The plain was a howling sea of dust.

"No stage?" she gasped.

The man laughed and shook his head. "There's the road. Injuns walk." He went on with his baggage-truck, and did not look at her again. He had not spoken unkindly: the fact and his blunt way of putting it were equally a matter of course, Squaws who "beat" their way in on freight trains do not go out by stage.

Meta crept away in the lee of a pile of freight, and sat down to nurse her child. The infant, like herself, had taken harm from exposure to the cold; his head pas-

sages were stopped, and when he tried to
nurse he had to fight with suffocation and
hunger both, and threw himself back in the
visible act of screaming, but his hoarse little
pipe was muted to a squeak.   This, which
sounds grotesque in the telling, was acute
anguish for the mother to see. She covered
her face with her blanket and sobbed and
coughed, and the pain tore her like a knife.
But she rose, and began her journey. She
had little conception of what she was under-
taking, but it would have made no difference; she must get there on her feet, since
there was no other way.

She no longer carried her baby squaw
fashion. She was out of sight of the station, and she hugged it where the burden
lay heaviest, on her heart. Her hands were
not free, but she had cast away her bundle
of food ; she could eat no more ; and the
warmth of the child's nestling body gave her
all the strength she had, — that and her
certainty of Henniker's welcome. That he
would be faithful to her presence she never
doubted. He would see her coming, perhaps, and he would run to catch her and the
child together in his arms. She could feel

the thrill of his eyes upon her, and the half
groan of joy with which he would strain her
to his breast. Then she would take one
deep, deep breath of happiness, — ah, that
pain! — and let the anguish of it kill her if
it must.

The snows on the mountains had come
down and encompassed the whole plain;
the winter's siege had begun. The winds
were iced to the teeth, and they smote like
armed men. They encountered Meta carrying some hidden, precious thing to the
garrison at Custer; they seized her and
searched her rudely, and left her, trembling
and disheveled, sobbing along with her silly
treasure in her arms. The dust rose in
columns, and traveled with mocking becks
and bows before her, or burst like a bomb
in her face, or circled about her like a band
of wild horses lashed by the hooting winds.

Meantime, Henniker, in span-new civil-
ian dress, was rattling across the plain on
the box seat of the ambulance, beside the
soldier driver. The ambulance was late to
catch the east-bound train, and the pay-
master was inside; so the four stout mules
laid back their ears and traveled, and the

heavy wheels bounded from stone to stone of the dust-buried road. Henniker smoked hard in silence, and drew great breaths of cold air into his splendid lungs. He was warm and clean and sound and fit, from top to toe. He had been drinking bounteous farewells to a dozen good comrades, and though sufficiently himself for all ordinary purposes, he was not that self he would have wished to be had he known that one of the test moments of his life was before him. It was a mood with him of headlong, treacherous quiet, and the devil of all foolish desires was showing him the pleasures of the world. He was in dangerously good health; he had got his discharge, and was off duty and off guard, all at once. He was a free man, though married. He was going to his wife, of course. Poor little Meta! God bless the girl, how she loved him! Ah, those black-eyed girls, with narrow temples and sallow, deep-fringed eyelids, they knew how to love a man! He was going to her by way of Laramie, or perhaps the coast. He might run upon a good thing over there, and start a bit of a home before he sent for her or went to fetch her; it was all one. She rested lightly on his mind, and he thought of her with a tender, reminiscent sadness, — rather a curious feeling considering that he was to see her now so soon. Why was she always " poor little Meta " in his thoughts ?

Poor little Meta was toiling on, for " Injuns walk." The dreadful pain of coughing was incessant. The dust blinded and choked her, and there was a roaring in her ears which she confused with the night and day burden of the trains. She was in a burning fever that was fever and chill in one, and her mind was not clear, except on the point of keeping on ; for once down, she felt that she could never get up again. At times she fancied she was clinging to the rocking, roaring platforms she had ridden on so long. The dust swirled around her — when had she breathed anything but dust ! The ground swam like water under her feet. She swayed, and seemed to be falling, — perhaps she did fall. But she was up and on her feet, the blanket cast from her head, when the ambulance drove straight towards her, and she saw him —

She had seen it coming, the ambulance, down the long, dizzy rise. The hills above

were white as death; a crooked gash of
color rent the sky; the toothed pines stood
black against that gleam, and through the
ringing in her ears, loud and sweet, she
heard the trumpets call. The cloud of de-
lirium lifted, and she saw the uniform she
loved; and beside the soldier driver sat her
white chief, looking down at her who came
so late with joy, bringing her babe, — her
sheaves, the harvest of that year's wild sow-
ing. But he did not seem to see her. She
had not the power to speak or cry. She
took one step forward and held up the child.

Then she fell down on her face in the
road, for the beloved one had seen her, and
had not known her, and had passed her by.
And God would not let her make one sound.

How in Heaven's name could it have happened! Could any man believe it of himself? Henniker put it to his reason, not to
speak of conscience or affection, and never
could explain, even to himself, that most unhappy moment of his life. If he had not a
heart for any helpless thing in trouble, who
had? He was the joke of the garrison for
his softness about dogs and women and children. Yet he had met his wife and baby on

the open road, and passed them by, and owned them not, and still he called himself a man.

What he had seen at first had been the abject figure of a little squaw facing the wind, her bowed head shrouded in her blanket, carrying something which her short arms could barely meet around, — a shapeless bundle. He did not think it a child, for a squaw will pack her baby always on her back. He had looked at her indifferently, but with condescending pity; for the day was rough, and the road was long, even for a squaw. Then, in all the disfigurement of her dirt and wretchedness and wild attire, it broke upon him that this creature was his wife, the rightful sharer of his life and freedom; and that animal-like thing she held up, that wrung its face and squeaked like a blind kitten, was his son.

Good God! He clutched the driver's arm, and the man swore and jerked his mules out of the road, for the woman had stopped right in the track where the wheels were going. The driver looked back, but could not see her; he knew that he had not touched her, only with the wind of his pace,

so he pulled the mules into the road again,
and the ambulance rolled on.

"Stop; let me get off. That woman is
my wife." Henniker heard himself saying
the words, but they were never spoken to
the ear. "Stop; let me get down," the inner voice prompted; but he did not make
a sound, and the curtains flapped and the
wheels went bounding along. They were a
long way past the spot, and the station was
in sight, when Henniker was heard to say
hoarsely, "Pick her up, as you go back, can't
you?"

"Pick up which?" asked the driver.

"The — that woman we passed just now."

"I'll see how she's making it," the man
answered coolly. "I ain't much stuck on
squaws. Acted like she was drunk or
crazy."

Henniker's face flushed, but he shuddered
as if he were cold.

"Pick her up, for the child's sake, by
God!" No man was ever more ashamed of
himself than he as he took out a gold piece
and handed it to the soldier. "Give her
this, Billy, — from yourself, you know. I
ain't in it."

Billy looked at Henniker, and then at the gold piece.   It was a double eagle ; all that the husband had dared to offer as alms to his wife, but more than enough to arouse the suspicions that he feared.

" Ain't in it, eh ? " thought the soldier. " You knew the woman, and she knew you. This is conscience money." But aloud he said, " A fool and his money are soon parted.   How do you know but I 'll blow it in at canteen ? "

" I 'll trust you," said Henniker.

The men did not speak to each other again.

" She 's one of them Bannocks that camped by old Pop Meadows's place, down at Bisuka, I bet," said the soldier to himself.

Henniker went on fighting his fight as if it had not been lost forever in that instant's hesitation.   A man cannot bethink himself : " By the way, it strikes me that was my wife and child we passed on the road ! " What he had done could never be explained without grotesque lying which would deceive nobody.

It could not be undone ; it must be lived down.   Henniker was much better at living

things down than he was at explaining or
trying to mend them.

After all, it was the girl's own fault, putting up that wretched squaw act on him.
To follow him publicly, and shame him
before all the garrison, in that beastly Bannock rig! Had she turned Bannock altogether and gone back to the tribe? In that
case let the tribe look after her; he could
have no more to do with her, of course.

He stepped into the smoking-car, and lost
himself as quickly as possible in the interest
of new faces around him, and the agreeable
impressions of himself which he read in eyes
that glanced and returned for another look
at so much magnificent health and color and
virility. His spot of turpitude did not show
through. He was still good to look at; and
to look the man that one would be goes a
long way toward feeling that one is that
man.

II

It was at Laramie, between the mountains, and Henniker was celebrating the
present and drowning the past in a large,
untrammeled style, when he received a letter
from the quartermaster-sergeant at Custer,

—a plain statement until the end, where Henniker read : —

"If you should happen at any time to wish for news of your son, Meadows and his wife have taken the child. They came on here to get him, and Meadows insisted on standing the expense of the funeral, which was the best we could give her for the credit of the troop. He put a handsome stone over her, with 'Meta, wife of Trumpeter Henniker, K Troop, —th U. S. Cavalry,' on it ; and there it stands to her memory, poor girl, and to your shame, a false, cruel, and cowardly man in the way you treated her. And so every one of us calls you, officers and men the same, — of your old troop that walked behind her to her grave. And where were you, Henniker, and what were you doing this day two weeks, when we were burying your poor wife ? The twenty dollars you sent her by Billy, Meadows has, and says he will keep it till he sees you again. Which some of us think it will be a good while he will be packing that Judas piece around with him. — And so good-by, Henniker. I might have said less, or I might have said nothing at all, but that the boy is

a fine child, my wife says, and must have
a grand constitution to stand what he has
stood; and I have a fondness for you myself when all is said and done.

"P. S. I would take a thought for that
boy once in a while, if I was you. A man
doesn't care for the brats when he is young,
but age cures us of all wants but the want
of a child."

But Henniker was not ready to go back
to the Meadows cottage and be clothed in
the robe of forgiveness, and receive his babe
like a pledge of penitence on his hand.

The shock of the letter sobered him at
first, and then the sting of it drove him to
drinking harder than ever. He did not run
upon that "good thing" at Laramie, nor in
any of the cities westward that one after
another beheld the progress of his deteriora-
tion. It does not take long in the telling,
but it was several years before he finally
struck upon the "Barbary Coast" in San
Francisco, where so many mothers' sons who
never were heard of have gone down. He
went ashore, but he did not quite go to
pieces. His constitution had matured under
healthy conditions, and could stand a good

deal of ill-usage ; but we are " no stronger
than our weakest part," and at the end of
all he found himself in a hospital bed under
treatment for his knee, — the same that
had been mulcted for him twice before.

He listened grimly to the doctor's expla-
nations, — how the past sins of his whole
impenitent system were being vicariously
reckoned for through this one afflicted member. It was rough on his old knee, Henniker remarked : but he had hopes of getting
out all right again, and he made the usual
sick-bed promises to himself. He did get
out, eventually, without a penny in the
world, and with a stiff knee to drag about
for the rest of his life. And he was just
thirty-four years old.

His splendid vitality, that had been wont
to express itself in so many attractive ways,
now found its chief vent in talk — inex-
pensive, inordinate, meddlesome discourse —
wherever two or three were gathered together
in the name of idleness and discontent.
The members of these congregations were
pessimists to a man. They disbelieved in
everybody and everything except themselves,
and secretly, at times, they were even a little

shaken on that head; but all the louder they exclaimed upon the world that had refused them the chance to be the great and successful characters nature had intended them to be.

It need hardly be said that when Henniker raved about the inequalities of class, the helplessness of poverty, the tyranny of wealth, and the curse of labor; and devoted in eloquent phrases the remainder of a blighted existence to the cause of the Poor Man, he was thinking of but one poor man, namely, himself. He classed himself with Labor only that he might feel his superiority to the laboring masses. There were few situations in which he could taste his superiority, in these days. The "ego" in his Cosmos was very hungry; his memories were bitter, his hopes unsatisfied; his vanity and artistic sense were crucified through poverty, lameness, and bad clothes. Now all that was left him was the conquests of the mind. For the smiles of women, give him the hoarse plaudits of men. The dandy of the garrison began to shine in saloon coteries and primaries of the most primary order. He was the star of sidewalk convocations and vacant-lot meetings of the Unemployed. But he despised the mob that echoed his perorations and paid for his drinks, and was at heart the aristocrat that his old uniform had made him.

In the summer of 1894, a little black-eyed boy with chestnut curls used to swing on the gate of the Meadows cottage that opens upon the common, and chant some verses of domestic doggerel about Coxey's army, which was then begging and bullying its way eastward, and demanding transportation at the expense of the railroads and of the people at large.

He sang his song to the well-marked tune of Pharaoh's Army, and thus the verses ran : —

> " The Coxeyites they gathered,
> The Coxeyites they gathered,
> And stole a train of freight-cars in the morn,
> And stole a train of freight-cars in the morning,
> And stole a train of freight-cars in the morn.
>
> " The engine left them standing,
> The engine left them standing,
> On the railroad-track at Caldwell in the morn.
> Very sad it was for Caldwell in the morning
> To feed that hungry army in the morn.

" Where are all the U. S. marshals,
    The deputy U. S. marshals,
To jail that Coxey army in the morn,
That 'industrious, law-abiding' Coxey's army
That stole a train of freight-cars in the morn ? "

Where indeed were all the U. S. marshals ? The question was being asked with
anxiety in the town, for a posse of them
had gone down to arrest the defiant train-
stealers, and it was rumored that the civil
arm had been disarmed, and the deputies
carried on as prisoners to Pocatello, where
the Industrials, two hundred strong, were
intrenched in the sympathies of the town,
and knocking the federal authorities about
at their law-abiding pleasure. Pocatello is
a division town on the Union Pacific Railroad ; it is full of the company's shops and
men, the latter all in the American Railway
Union or the Knights of Labor, and solid on
class issues, right or wrong ; and it was said
that the master workman was expected at
Pocatello to speak on the situation, and, if
need arose, to call out the trades all over
the land in support of the principle that
tramp delegations shall not walk. Disquiet-
ing rumors were abroad, and there was
relief in the news that the regulars had been

called on to sustain the action of the federal court.

The troops at Bisuka barracks were under marching orders. While the town was alert to hear them go they tramped away one evening, just as a shower was clearing that had emptied the streets of citizens; and before the ladies could say " There they go," and call each other to the window, they were gone.

Then for a few days the remote little capital, with Coxeyites gathering and threatening its mails and railroad service, waited in apprehensive curiosity as to what was going to happen next. The party press on both sides seized the occasion to point a moral on their own account, and some said, " Behold the logic of McKinleyism," and others retorted, " Behold the shadow of the Wilson Bill stalking abroad over the land. Let us fall on our faces and pray!" But most people laughed instead, and patted the Coxeyites on the back, preferring their backs to their faces.

It seemed as if it might be time to stop laughing and gibing and inviting the procession to move on, when a thousand or more men, calling themselves American citizens, were parading their idleness through the land as authority for lawlessness and crime, and when our sober regulars had to be called out to quell a Falstaff's army. The regulars, be sure, did not enjoy it. If there is a sort of service our soldiers would like to be spared, doubtless it is disarming crazy Indians : but they prefer even that to standing up to be stoned and insulted and chunked with railroad iron by a mob which they are ordered not to fire upon, or to entering a peaceful country which has been sown with dynamite by patriotic labor unions, or prepared with cut - bridges by sympathetic strikers.

We are here to be hurt, so the strong ones tell us, and perhaps the best apology the strong can make to the weak for the vast superiority that training gives is to show how long they can hold their fire amidst a mob of brute ignorances, and how much better they can bear their hurts when the senseless missiles fly. We love the forbearance of our " unpitied strong ; " it is what we expect of them : but we trust also in their firmness when the time for forbearance is past.

Little Ross Henniker — named for that mythical great Scotchman, his supposed grandfather — was deeply disappointed because he did not see the soldiers go. To have lived next door to them all his life, seven whole years, and watched them practicing and preparing to be fit and ready to go, and then not to see them when they did march away for actual service in the field, was hard indeed.

Ross was not only one of those brightest boys of his age known to parents and grandparents by the million, but he was really a very bright and handsome child. If Mother Meadows, now "granny," had ever had any doubts at all about the Scottish chief of the Hudson's Bay Company, the style and presence of that incomparable boy were proof enough. It was a marked case of "throwing-back." There was none of the Bannock here. Could he not be trusted like a man to do whatever things he liked to do; as riding to fetch the cows and driving them hillward again, on the weird little spotted pony, hardly bigger than a dog, with a huge head and a furry cheek and a hanging under-lip, which the tributary Bannocks had brought him?

It was while he was on cow-duty far away,
but not out of sight of the post, that he saw
the column move. "Great Scott!" how he
did ride! He broke his stick over the pony's
back, and kicked him with his bare heels,
and slapped him with his hat, till the pony
bucked him off into a sagebush whence he
picked himself up and flew as fast as his own
legs would spin; but he was too late. Then,
for the first time in six months at least, he
howled. Aunt Callie comforted him with
fresh strawberry jam for supper, but the
lump of grief remained, until, as she was
washing the dishes, she glanced at him,
laughing out of the corner of her eye, and
began to make up the song about Coxey's
army. For some time Ross refused to smile,
but when it came to the chorus about the soldiers who were going

" To turn back Coxey's army, hallelujah!
To turn back Coxey's army, halleloo!"

he began to sing "hallelujah" too. Then
gun-fire broke in with a lonesome sound, as
if the cavalry up on the hill missed its comrades of the white stripes who were gone to
" turn back " that ridiculous army.

Mother Meadows wished "that man Coxey had never been born," so weary did she get of the Coxey song. Coxeyism had taken complete possession of the young lord of the house, now that his friends the soldiers had gone to take a hand in the business.

In a few days the soldiers came back escorting the Coxey prisoners. The "presence of the troops" had sufficed. The two hundred Coxeyites were to be tried at Bisuka for crimes committed within the State. They were penned meanwhile in a field by the river, below the railroad track, and at night they were shut into a rough barrack which had been hastily put up for the purpose. A skirt of the town little known, except to the Chinese vegetable gardeners and makers of hay on the river meadows and small boys fishing along the shore, now became the centre of popular regard; and "Have you been down to the Coxey camp?" was as common a question as "Are you going to the Natatorium Saturday night?" or "Will there be a mail from the west to-day?"

One evening, Mother Meadows, with little Ross Henniker by the hand, stood close to the dead-line of the Coxey field, watching

the groups on the prisoners' side. The woman looked at them with perplexed pity, but
the child swung himself away and cried,
" Pooh ! only a lot of dirty hobos ! " and
turned to look at the soldiers.

The tents of the guard of regulars stood
in a row in front of a rank of tall poplar-
trees, their tops swinging slow in the last
sunlight. Behind the trees stretched the
green river flats in the shadow. Frogs were
croaking; voices of girls could be heard in a
tennis-court with a high wall that ran back
to the street of the railroad.

Roll-call was proceeding in front of the
tents, the men firing their quick, harsh answers like scattering shots along the line.
Under the trees at a little distance the beautiful sleek cavalry horses were grouped, un-
saddled and calling for their supper. Ross
Henniker gazed at them with a look of joy;
then he turned a contemptuous eye upon the
prisoners.

" Which of them two kinds of animals
looks most like what a man ought to be? " he
asked, pointing to the horses and then to the
Coxeyites, who in the cool of the evening were
indulging in unbeautiful horse-play, not with-

out a suspicion of showing off before the eyes of visitors. The horses in their free impatience were as unconscious as lords.

"What are you saying, Ross?" asked Mrs. Meadows, rousing herself.

"I say, suppose I'd just come down from the moon, or some place where they don't know a man from a horse, and you said to me: 'Look at these things, and then look at them things over there, and say which is boss of t' other.' Why, I'd say *them* things, every time." Ross pointed without any prejudice to the horses.

"My goodness!" cried Mrs. Meadows, "if these Coxeys had been taken care of and coddled all their lives like them troop horses, they might not be so handsome, but they'd look a good deal better than what they do. And they'd have more sense," she added in a lower voice. "Very few poor men's sons get the training those horses have had. They've learned to mind, for one thing, and to be faithful to the hand that feeds them."

"Not all of them don't," said Ross, shaking his head wisely. "There's kickers and biters and shirks amongst them; but if they

won't learn and can't learn, they get 'condemned.'"

"And what becomes of them then?"

"Why, *you* know," answered the boy,
who began to suspect that there was a
moral looming in the distance of this bold
generalization.

"Yes," said Mother Meadows, "I know
what becomes of some of them, because I've
seen; and I don't think a condemned horse
looks much better in the latter end of him
than a condemned man."

"But you can't leave them in the troop,
for they'd spoil all the rest," objected the
boy.

"It's too much for me, dear," replied the
old woman humbly. "These Coxeys are a
kind of folks I don't understand."

"I should think you might understand,
when the troops have to go out and run 'em
in! I'm on the side of the soldiers, every
time."

"Well, that's simple enough," said Mrs.
Meadows. She was a very mild protago-
nist, for she could never confine herself to
one side of a question. "I'm on the side
of the soldiers, too. A soldier has to do

what he 's told, and pays with his life for it, right or wrong."

" And I think it 's a shame to send the beautiful clean soldiers to shove a lot of dirty hobos back where they belong."

" My goodness! Hush! you 'd better talk less till you get more sense to talk with," said Mrs. Meadows sternly. A man standing near, with his back to them, had turned around quickly, and she saw by his angry eye that he had overheard. She looked at him again, and knew the man. It was the boy's father. Ross had bounded away to talk to his friend Corporal Niles.

" Henniker! " exclaimed Mrs. Meadows in a low voice of shocked amazement. " It don't seem as if this could be you! "

" Let that be! " said Henniker roughly. " I did n't enlist by that name in this army. Who 's that young son of a gun that 's got so much lip on him? "

" God help you! don't you know your own son? "

" What? No! Has he got to be that size already? " The man's weather-beaten face turned a darker red under the week-old beard that disfigured it. He sat down on the ground, for suddenly he felt weak, and also to hide his lameness from the woman who should have hated him, but who simply pitied him instead. Her face showed a sort of motherly shame for the change that she saw in him. It was very hard to bear. He had not fully realized the change in himself till its effect upon her confronted him. He tried to bluff it off carelessly.

" Bring the boy here. I have a word to say to him."

" You should have said it long ago, then." Mrs. Meadows was hurt and indignant at his manner. " What has been said is said, for good and all. It's too late to unsay it now."

" What do you mean by that, Mrs. Meadows ? Am I the boy's father or am I not ? "

" You are not thefather he knows. Do you think I have been teaching him to be ashamed of the name he bears ? "

" Old lady," cried Henniker the Coxeyite, " have you been stuffing that boy about his dad as you did the mother about hers ? "

" I have told him the truth, partly. The rest, if it wasn't the truth, it ought to have been," answered Mrs. Meadows stoutly. "I have put the story right, as an honest man would have lived it. Whatever you've been doing with yourself these years, it's your own affair, not the boy's nor mine. Keep it to yourself now. You were too good for them once, — the mother and the child; they can do without you now."

"That's all right," said Henniker, wincing; "but as a matter of curiosity let me hear how you have put it up."

"How I have what?"

"How you have dressed up the story to the boy. I'd like to see myself with a woman's eyes once more."

Mrs. Meadows looked him over and hesitated; then her face kindled. "I've told him that his father was a beautiful clean man," she said, using unconsciously the boy's own words, "and rode a beautiful horse, and saluted his captain so!" She pointed to the corporal of the guard who was at that moment reporting. "I told him that when the troops went you had to leave your young wife behind you, and she could not be kept from following you with her child; and by a cruel mischance you passed each other on

the road, and you never knew till you had
got to her old home and heard she was dead
and buried; and you were so broke up that
you could n't bear your life in the place
where you used to be with her; and you
were a sorrowful wandering man that he
must pray for, and ask God to bring you
home.　You never came near us, Henniker,
nor thought of coming; but could I tell your
own child that?　Indeed, I would be afraid
to tell him what did happen on that road
from Custer station, for fear when he 's a
man he 'd go hunting you with a shotgun.
Now where is the falsehood here?　Is it in
me, or in you, who have made it as much as
your own life is worth to tell the truth
about you to your son?　*Was* it the truth,
Henniker?　Sure, man, you did love her!
What did you want with her else?　Was
it the truth that they told us at Custer?
There are times when I can't believe it myself.　If there is a word you could say for
yourself, — say it, for the child's sake!
You would n't mind speaking to an old
woman like me?　There was a time when I
would have been proud to call you my son."

"You are a good woman, Mrs. Meadows,

but I cannot lie to you, even for the child's
sake. And it's not that I don't know how
to lie, for God knows I'm nothing but a lie
this blessed minute! What do I care for
such cattle as these?" He had risen, and
waved his hand contemptuously toward his
fellow-martyrs. "Well, I must be going.
I see they're passin' around the flesh-pots.
We're livin' like fighting-cocks here, on a
restaurant contract. There'll be a big deal
in it for the marshal, I suspect." Henniker
winked, and his face fell into the lowest of
its demoralized expressions.

"There's no such a thing!" said Mrs.
Meadows indignantly. "Some folks are
willing to work for very little these hard
times, and give good value for their money.
You had better eat and be thankful, and
leave other folks alone!"

Little Ross coming up heard but the last
words, and saw his granny's agitation and
the familiar attitude of the strange Coxeyite. His quick temper flashed out: "Get
out with you! Go off where you belong,
you dirty man!"

Mrs. Meadows caught the boy, and
whirled him around and shook him.

" Never, never let me hear you speak like
that to any man again ! ' ''

" Why ? " he demanded.

" I 'll tell you why, some day, if I have
to.   Pray God I may never need to tell
you ! ''

" Why ? " repeated the boy, wondering
at her excitement.

" Come away, — come away home ! " she
said, and Ross saw that her eyes were red
with unshed tears.   He hung behind her
and looked back.

" He 's lame," said he, half to himself.
" I would n't have spoken that way if I 'd
known he had a game leg."

" Who 's lame ? " asked Mrs. Meadows.

" The Coxeyite.   See.   He limps bad."

" Did n't I tell you !   We never know,
when we call names, what sore spots we
may be hitting.   You may have sore spots
of your own some day."

" I hope I sha'n't be lame," mused the
boy.   " And I hope I sha'n't be a Coxey."

The Coxeyites had been in camp a fort-
night when their trial began.   Twice a
day the prisoners were marched up the
streets of Bisuka to the court-house, and

back again to camp, till the citizens became accustomed to the strange, unrepubli-
can procession. The prisoners were herded
along the middle of the street; on either
side of them walked the marshals, and outside of the line of civil officers the guard of
infantry or cavalry, the officers riding and
the men on foot.

This was the last march of the Coxeyites.
Many citizens looking on were of the opinion that if these men desired to make themselves an "object-lesson" to the nation, this
was their best chance of being useful in
that capacity.

For two weeks, day by day, in the prisoner's field, Henniker had been confronted
with the contrast of his old service with his
present demoralization. He had been a
conspicuous figure among the Industrials
until they came in contact with the troops;
then suddenly he subsided, and was heard
and seen as little as possible. Not for all
that a populist congress could vote, out of
the pockets of the people into the pockets of
the tramp petitioners, would he have posed
as one of them before the eyes of an officer,
or a man, of his old regiment. who might

remember him as Trumpeter Henniker of K troop. But the daily march to the court-house was the death-sickness of his pride. Once he had walked these same streets with his head as high as any man's ; and it had been, " How are you, Henniker ? " and " Step in, Henniker ; " or Callie had been laughing and falling out of step on his arm, or Meta — poor little Meta — waiting for him when the darkness fell!

Now the women ran to the windows and crowded the porches, and stared at him and his ill-conditioned comrades as if they had been animals belonging to a different species.

But Henniker was mistaken here. The eyes of the pretty girls were for the " pretty soldiers." It was all in the day's work for the soldiers, who tramped indifferently along ; but the officers looked bored, as if they were neither proud of the duty nor of the display of it which the times demanded.

On the last day's march from the court-house to the camp, there was a clamor of voices that drowned the shuffling and tramp-ing of the feet. The prisoners were all talking at once, discussing the sentences which the court had just announced: the leaders and those taken in acts of violence to be imprisoned at hard labor for specified terms; the rank and file to be put back on their stolen progress as far westward, whence they came, as the borders of the State would allow; there to be staked out, as it were, on the banks of the Snake River, and guarded for sixty days by the marshals, supported by the inevitable "presence of the troops."

But the sentence that Henniker heard was that private one which his own child had spoken: "Get out with you! Go back where you belong, you dirty man!" He had wished at the time that he could make the proud youngster feel the sting of his own lash: but that thought had passed entirely, and been merged in the simple hurt of a father's longing for his son. "If he were mine," he bitterly confessed, "if that little cock-a-hoop rascal would own me and love me for his dad, I swear to God I could begin my life again! But now, what next?"

There had been a stoppage ahead, the feet pressing on had slackened step, when there, with his back to the high iron gates of

the capitol-grounds, was the beautiful child
again. A young woman stood beside him,
a fine, wholesome girl like a full-blown cottage rose, with auburn hair, an ivory-white
throat, and a back as flat as a trooper's. It
was Callie, of course, with Meta's child. The
cup of Henniker's humilation was full.

The boy stood with his chin up, his hat
on the back of his head, his plump hands
spread on the hips of his white knicker-
bockers. He was dressed in his best, as he
had come from a children's fête. Around
his neck hung a prize which he had won in
the games, a silver dog-whistle on a scarlet
ribbon. He caught it to his lips and blew
a long piercing trill, his dark eyes smiling,
the wind blowing the short curls across his
cheek.

" There he is, the lame one ! I made
him look round," said Ross.

Henniker had turned, for one long look
— the last, he thought — at his son. All
the singleness and passion of the mother,
the fire and grace and daring of the father,
were in the promise of his childish face and
form. He flushed, not a self-conscious, but
an honest, generous blush, and took his hat

away off his head to the lame Coxeyite —
" because I was mean to him ; and they are
down and done for now, the Coxeys."

" Whose kid is that?" asked the man
who walked beside Henniker, seeing the
gesture and the look that passed between
the man and the boy. " He's as handsome
as they make 'em," he added, smiling.

Henniker did not reply in the proud
word " Mine." A sudden heat rushed to
his eyes, his chest was tight to bursting.
He pulled his hat down and tramped along.
The shuffling feet of the prisoners passed on
down the middle of the street; the double
line of guards kept step on either side. The
dust arose and blended the moving shapes,
prisoners and guards together, and blotted
them out in the distance.

Callie had not seen her old lover at all.
" Great is the recuperative power of the
human heart." She had been looking at
Corporal Niles, who could not turn his well-
drilled head to look at her. But a side-
spark from his blue eye shot out in her
direction, and made her blush and cease to
smile. Corporal Niles carried his head a
little higher and walked a little straighter

after that; and Callie went slowly through
the gates, and sat a long while on one of the
benches in the park, with her elbow resting
on the iron scroll and her cheek upon her
hand.

She was thinking about the Coxeyites'
sentence, and wondering if the cavalry would
have to go down to the stockade prison on
the Snake; for in that case Corporal Niles
would have to go, and the wedding be post-
poned. Everybody knows it is bad luck to
put off a wedding-day; and besides, the yellow roses she had promised her corporal to
wear would all be out of bloom, and no other
roses but those were the true cavalry yellow.

But the cavalry did not go down till
after the wedding, which took place on the
evening appointed, at the Meadows cottage,
between "Sound off" and "Taps." The
ring was duly blessed, and the father's and
mother's kiss was not wanting. The primrose radiance of the summer twilight shone
as strong as lamplight in the room, and
Callie, in her white dress, with her auburn
braids gleaming through the wedding-veil
and her lover's colors in the roses on her

breast, was as sweet and womanly a picture as any mother could wish to behold.

When little Ross came up to kiss the bride, he somehow forgot, and flung his arms first around Corporal Niles's brown neck.

"Corporal, I'm twice related to the cavalry now," said he. "I had a father in it, and now I've got an uncle in it."

"That's right," the corporal agreed; "and if you have any sort of luck you'll be in it yourself some day."

"But not in the ranks," said Ross firmly. "I'm going to West Point, you know."

"Bless his heart!" cried Callie, catching the boy in her arms; "and how does he think he's going to get there?"

"I shall manage it somehow," said Ross, struggling. He was very fond of Aunt Callie, but a boy doesn't like to be hugged so before his military acquaintances, and in Ross's opinion there had been a great deal too much kissing and hugging, not to speak of crying, already. He did not see why there should be all this fuss just because Aunt Callie was going up to the barracks to live, in the jolliest little whitewashed cabin,

with a hop-vine hanging, like the veil on an
old woman's bonnet, over the front gable.
He only wished that the corporal had asked
him to go too!

A slight misgiving about his last speech
was making Ross uncomfortable. If there
was a person whose feelings he would not
have wished to hurt for anything in the
world, it was Corporal Niles.

" Corporal," he amended affectionately,
" if I should be a West Pointer, and should
be over you, I should n't put on any airs,
you know. We should be better friends
than ever."

" I expect we should, captain. I 'm looking forward to the day."

A mild species of corvée had been put in
force down on the Snake River while the
stockade prison was building. The prisoners
as a body rebelled against it, and were not
constrained to work ; but a few were willing, and these were promptly stigmatized as
" scabs," and ill treated by the lordly idlers.
Hence they were given a separate camp and
treated as trusties.

When the work was done the trusties

were rewarded with their freedom, either to go independently, or to stay and eat government rations till the sixty days of their sentence had expired.

Henniker, in spite of his infirmity, had been one of the hardest volunteer workers. But now the work was done, and the question returned, What next? What comes after Coxeyism when Coxeyism fails?

He sat one evening by the river, and again he was a free man. A dry embankment, warm as an oven to the touch, sloped up to the railroad track above his head; tufts of young sage and broken stone strewed the face of it; there was not a tree in sight. He heard the river boiling down over the rapids and thundering under the bridge. He heard the trumpets calling the men to quarters. "Lights out" had sounded some time before. He had been lying motionless, prone on his face, his head resting on his crossed arms. The sound of the trumpets made him choke up like a homesick boy. He lay there till, faintly in the distance, "Taps" breathed its slow and sweet good-night.

" Last call," he said. " Time to turn in."

He rolled over and began to pull off the rags in which his child had spurned him.

" The next time I 'm inspected," he muttered, "I shall be a clean man." So, naked, he slipped into the black water under the bank. The river bore him up and gave him one. more chance, but he refused it : with two strokes he was in the midst of the death-current, and it seized him and took him down.

Clara Louise Burnham.

Young Maids and Old. 16mo, $1.25; paper, 50 cents.
Next Door. 16mo, $1.25; paper, 50 cents.
Dearly Bought. 16mo, $1.25.
No Gentlemen. 16mo, $1.25; paper, 50 cents.
A Sane Lunatic. 16mo, $1.25; paper, 50 cents.
The Mistress of Beech Knoll. 16mo, $1.25; paper, 50 cents.
Miss Bagg's Secretary. 16mo, $1.25.
Dr. Latimer. 16mo, $1.25.
Sweet Clover: A Romance of the White City. 16mo, $1.25.
The Wise Woman. 16mo, $1.25.

Edwin Lassetter Bynner.

Zachary Phips. 16mo, $1.25; paper, 50 cents.
Agnes Surriage. 16mo, $1.25; paper, 50 cents.
The Begum's Daughter. 12mo, $1.25.
  These three Historical Novels, 16mo, in box, $3.75.
Penelope's Suitors. 24mo, boards, 50 cents.
Damen's Ghost. 16mo, $1.00; paper, 50 cents.
An Uncloseted Skeleton. (Written with Lucretia P. Hale.) 32mo, 50 cents.

Rose Terry Cooke.

Somebody's Neighbors. Stories. 12mo, $1.25; half calf, $3.00; paper, 50 cents.
Happy Dodd. 12mo, $1.25.
The Sphinx's Children. Stories. 12mo, $1.25.
Steadfast. 12mo, $1.25; paper, 50 cents.
Huckleberries. Gathered from New England Hills. Short Stories. 16mo, $1.25.

Charles Egbert Craddock [Mary N. Murfree].

In the Tennessee Mountains. Short Stories. 16mo, $1.25.
Down the Ravine. For Young People. Illustrated. 16mo, $1.00.
The Prophet of the Great Smoky Mountains. 16mo, $1.25.
In the Clouds. 16mo, $1.25.
The Story of Keedon Bluffs. 16mo, $1.00.
The Despot of Broomsedge Cove. 16mo, $1.25.
Where the Battle was Fought. 16mo, $1.25.
His Vanished Star. 16mo, $1.25.
The Mystery of Witch-Face Mountain, and Other Stories. 16mo, $1.25.

Oliver Wendell Holmes.

Elsie Venner. Crown 8vo, $1.50; paper, 50 cents.
The Guardian Angel. Crown 8vo, $1.50; paper, 50 cents.
A Mortal Antipathy. Crown 8vo, $1.50.

Augustus Hoppin.

Recollections of Auton House. Illustrated by the
Author. Square 8vo, $1.25.
A Fashionable Sufferer. Illustrated by the Author.
12mo, $1.50.
Two Compton Boys. Illustrated by the Author.
Square 8vo, $1.50.

Henry James.

Watch and Ward. 18mo, $1.25.
A Passionate Pilgrim, and other Tales. 12mo, $2.00.
Roderick Hudson. 12mo, $2.00.
The American. 12mo, $2.00.
The Europeans. 12mo, $1.50.
Confidence. 12mo, $1.50; paper, 50 cents.
The Portrait of a Lady. 12mo, $2.00.
The Author of Beltraffio; Pandora; Georgina's Rea-
sons; Four Meetings, etc. 12mo, $1.50.
The Siege of London; The Pension Beaurepas; and
The Point of View. 12mo, $1.50.
Tales of Three Cities (The Impressions of a Cousin;
Lady Barberina; A New-England Winter). 12mo,
$1.50; paper, 50 cents.
Daisy Miller: A Comedy. 12mo, $1.25.
The Tragic Muse. 2 vols. 16mo, $2.50.

Sarah Orne Jewett.

The King of Folly Island, and other People. 16mo, $1.25.
Tales of New England. In Riverside Aldine Series.
16mo, $1.00.
A White Heron, and Other Stories. 18mo, $1.25.
A Marsh Island. 16mo, $1.25; paper, 50 cents.
A Country Doctor. 16mo, $1.25; paper, 50 cents,
Deephaven. 18mo, gilt top, $1.25.
Old Friends and New. 18mo, gilt top, $1.25.
Country By-Ways. 18mo, gilt top, $1.25.
The Mate of the Daylight, and Friends Ashore. 18mo,
gilt top, $1.25.
Betty Leicester. 18mo, gilt top, $1.25.
Strangers and Wayfarers. 16mo, $1.25.
A Native of Winby. 16mo, $1.25.
The Life of Nancy, and Other Stories. 16mo, $1.25.

Ellen Olney Kirk.

The Story of Lawrence Garthe. 16mo, $1.25.
Ciphers. 16mo, $1.25; paper, 50 cents.
The Story of Margaret Kent. 16mo, $1.25; paper, 50 cents.
Sons and Daughters. 12mo, $1.25; paper, 50 cents.
Queen Money. 16mo, $1.25; paper, 50 cents.
Better Times. Stories. 12mo, $1.50.
A Midsummer Madness. 16mo, $1.25; paper, 50 cents.
A Lesson in Love. 16mo, $1.00; paper, 50 cents.
A Daughter of Eve. 12mo, $1.50; paper, 50 cents.
Walford. 16mo, $1.25; paper, 50 cents.

Elizabeth Stuart Phelps [Mrs. Ward].

The Gates Ajar. 16mo, $1.50.
Beyond the Gates. 16mo, $1.25.
The Gates Between. 16mo, $1.25.
Men, Women, and Ghosts. Stories. 16mo, $1.50.
Hedged In. 16mo, $1.50.
The Silent Partner. 16mo, $1.50.
The Story of Avis. 16mo, $1.50; paper, 50 cents.
Sealed Orders, and other Stories. 16mo, $1.50.
Friends: A Duet. 16mo, $1.25; paper, 50 cents.
Dr. Zay. 16mo, $1.25; paper, 50 cents.
An Old Maid's Paradise, and Burglars in Paradise. 16mo, $1.25.
The Master of the Magicians. Collaborated by Elizabeth Stuart Phelps and Herbert D. Ward. 16mo, $1.25; paper, 50 cents.
Come Forth. Collaborated by Elizabeth Stuart Phelps and Herbert D. Ward. 16mo, $1.25.
Fourteen to One. Short Stories. 16mo, $1.25.
Donald Marcy. 16mo, $1.25.
The Madonna of the Tubs. With Illustrations. Square 12mo, 75 cents.
Jack the Fisherman. Illustrated. Square 12mo, ornamental boards, 50 cents.
A Singular Life. 16mo, $1.25.

F. Hopkinson Smith.

Colonel Carter of Cartersville. With Illustrations. 16mo, $1.25.
A Day at Laguerre's, and other Days. 16mo, $1.25.
A Gentleman Vagabond, and other Stories. 16mo, $1.25.

Octave Thanet.
Knitters in the Sun.   16mo, $1.25.
Otto the Knight, and other Stories.   16mo, $1.25.

William Makepeace Thackeray.
Complete Works. *Illustrated Library Edition.* With
Biographical and Bibliographical Introductions, Portrait, and over 1600 Illustrations.   22 vols. crown
8vo, gilt top, each, $1.50.   The set, $33.00; half calf,
$60.50; half calf, gilt top, $65.00; half levant, $77.00.

Gen. Lew Wallace.
The Fair God; or, The Last of the 'Tzins.   A Tale of
the Conquest of Mexico.   12mo, $1.50.

Mrs. A. D. T. Whitney.
Faith Gartney's Girlhood.   16mo, $1.25.
Hitherto.   16mo, $1.25.
Patience Strong's Outings.   16mo, $1.25.
The Gayworthys.   16mo, $1.25.
A Summer in Leslie Goldthwaite's Life.   16mo, $1.25.
We Girls.   16mo, $1.25.
Real Folks.   16mo, $1.25.
The Other Girls.   16mo, $1.25.
Sights and Insights.   2 vols.   16mo, $2.50.
Odd or Even ?   16mo, $1.25.
Bonnyborough.   16mo, $1.25.
Homespun Yarns.   Stories.   16mo, $1.25.
Ascutney Street.   16mo, $1.25.
A Golden Gossip.   16mo, $1.25.
Boys at Chequasset.   16mo, $1.25.
Mother Goose for Grown Folks.   16mo, $1.25.

Kate Douglas Wiggin.
The Birds' Christmas Carol.   With illustrations. New
Edition.   Square 12mo, boards, 50 cents.
The Story of Patsy. Illustrated. Square 16mo, boards,
60 cents.
Timothy's Quest.   16mo, $1.00.
A Summer in a Cañon.   Illustrated.   16mo, $1.25.
A Cathedral Courtship, and Penelope's English Expe-
riences.   Illustrated,   16mo, $1.00.
Polly Oliver's Problem.   Illustrated.   16mo, $1.00.
The Story Hour.   Illustrated.   16mo, $1.00.
Timothy's Quest. *Holiday Edition.* Illustrated by
Oliver Herford.   12mo, $1.50.